The Greek Constellations - Virgo and Libra

The Greek Constellations - Virgo and Libra

Stephan De Jonghe

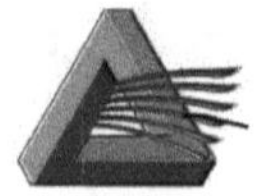

Contents

In the footsteps of Homer and Hesiod.

From Astronomy to Mythology

How the constellations came to be named by the Greek God's.

Stephan J De Jonghe

Novella Ten

The constellations of

Virgo and Libra

The story of Astraea the Maiden and Themis the Scales

Copyright

The Greek Constellations – Virgo and Libra

Copyright © 2025 by Stephan De Jonghe

For permission requests, write to the publisher at: stephansfolliclefarm@gmail.com

Ordering Information:
Special discounts are available on quantity purchases by book resellers, corporations, associations, and others. For details, contact the publisher at the email address above.

The Greek Constellations – Virgo and Libra
by Stephan De Jonghe
ISBN 978-1-7636516-6-1 (paperback)
ISBN 978-1-7636516-7-8 (Ebook)

Publisher
Stephan De Jonghe Publishing,
Hillarys, Perth, Western Australia, Australia 6025

Printer and distributor
Ingram Content Group
1 Ingram Blvd.
La Vergne, Tennessee USA 37086

The dedication.

To say that my darling wife is the love of my life
is an understatement.

Deb is my best friend, soul mate, confidant, and life partner.

Among so many other things, we also share a love of books, and
we have a massive library on display in our home of books that we
want to read.

Our topics include action, comedy, romance, science fiction,
crime, thrillers, and adventure.
We also have an impressive non-fiction collection.

My endeavours as an author represent a passion that
burns powerfully for me. I am driven to write.

I have many stories to tell and writing them and publishing them
is my way of contributing to other people's library's.

Writing involves many hours of research and then sitting in soli-
tude, slowly assembling the words that details a journey into a read-
able story. One that was only previously an idea.

This takes a lot of patience and persistence.
After the story is put down, the process of editing begins.

Few non-writers understand that this stage can take as much five times longer than it takes to write the actual first draft.

My Deb gives me the support that I need to execute my writing passion.
She not only supports my writing, but also enjoys reading the stories.

Her assistance with proof reading, feed-back on content, and editing, is invaluable.
Especially after I have become blind to my own errors.
She understands how important it is to me and to you, the reader, to get it right.

I dedicate these books to my wife as my thanks to her for her on-going support, and for her contributions to the finished publications.

We are a team.

We both hope that you enjoy this series of books, and we look forward to your feedback.

Stephan and Deb De Jonghe

Special thanks

My special thanks go to Janey Emery – Renowned Australian artist, for giving me permission to use her art for the covers for my Greek Constellation series of books.

"I hope you enjoy her art and the story within these pages."
Stephan De Jonghe - Author

Janey's Story - Born in Narrogin, Western Australia, Janey Emery's interest in art began as early as 2 years of age and led to art becoming the central element in Janey's Childhood. Excelling in art throughout her school years Janey devoted herself to the art course provided by Balcatta Senior High school, where her passion for art only intensified.

Janey has been painting fulltime since 1991 and has attained a high degree of respect in the art world from peers and art lovers alike. Janey has won numerous distinguished artistic awards for her work and has sold many paintings throughout Australia and overseas. Janey Emery is achieving the recognition her distinctive artistic talents deserve.

Janey is Self-Taught in All Mediums with the exception of leisure courses undertaken in oil and water colours.

"Art has always played a part of who I am. From early childhood to now there has been a need for me to express myself through drawing and painting. I find peace in my craft, and I hope I bring that to my paintings."

"To me, my Art is like breathing. Painting is my life."
Janey Emery - Artist
https://www.janeyemery.art/

Autor's note

Author's note: This story is based on Greek mythology. Virgo however, is the Latin name for Virgin or Maiden. Libra however, is the Latin name for Scales and associated with fairness and proportional balance. These two legends that form the star signs Virgo and Libra are entwined. The accounts of these two goddesses are relevant to each so I have chosen to portray the account of both Virgo and Libra as one story in order to achieve continuity. Unlike the other star sign constellations, the resource material for them is very scant and so this story is more from my imagination than a retelling of the existing mythology. I have included what I could learn from my research, but there was actually not much to work with....

Many of these stories owe some of their earlier history to the Phoenicians, Babylonians, and Mycenaean's, and were initially used to help ancient travellers remember star patterns as a nighttime navigational tool. Over time these fascinating stories were greatly embellished on how the constellations came to be formed. The ancient Greeks called these constellations the "Katasterismoi" meaning, "the placing of the stars." They gave names and told stories about forty-eight out of the eighty-eight constellations that are recognised by the International Astronomical Union.

These mythologies were embellished as they were countlessly re-told with tales of gods encountering wild creatures, fighting fierce battles, and of course, having lots of sex. After all, these men were away from home for lengthy periods of time. They shared these stories to entertain urban dwellers that they encountered, and from there the stories became legends, and for many people they became their religion.

A Greek poet and storyteller named Homer was the first person to document these stories and he is most famous for the "Iliad" and the "Odyssey" which he composed some 2,800 years ago. Whilst little is known about Homer, he is regarded by many as the founder of modern literature. His two main works were the first literary works to be taught formally to students. Interestingly, there are thirty-three film adaptations of the Odyssey, proving his works are still relevant to modern audiences.

Later, a poet named Hesiod, significantly contributed to Greek mythology and followed on from Homer's work. Together they are attributed with establishing ancient Greek religious customs, formal astronomy, the development of structured learning, documenting events, early economics, commercial farming, and time keeping.

The word "zodiac" originated from the Greek words "Zodiakos kuklos," meaning "circle of little animals". It wasn't until 50BCE that the first classical zodiac depicting the twelve astrological star signs in their current order was first depicted. It is known as the "Dendera zodiac."

During the 2nd century CE, a Greco-Roman astrologer and astronomer named Claudius Ptolemy worked on his documented Tetrabiblos into what is regarded as western astrology's primary source document and remains largely in use today. Also of note is that astronomers have named a crater on the Luna surface, and another on the surface of the planet Mars Ptolemaeus, in honour of Ptolemy and his contribution to astronomy.

The connection between Greek names and Roman names for the same deities came from their translation from one language to the other. In ancient Greek, Zeus is pronounced Dias. In Latin that became Djous Pater (Sky father) or Luppiter. In English this became Jupiter. Many names evolved in this way.

As an author, my goal is to turn what is known of the mythology, into an enjoyable story for today's reader.   *Stephan J De Jonghe*

Chronology

Yet another note from the author, Stephan De Jonghe

My "from astronomy to mythology" series of novellas posed some difficulties in terms of writing the stories into a logical chronology. Until the Iliad, and the Odessey, no one had ever written any of the tales of titan's forming the world, or their ultimate defeat by the gods who eventually resided in Mount Olympus. These stories were imagined piecemeal, embellished, refined, and retold over a thousand-year period. Unlike history, which did happen on a linear timeline and can be plotted, the timeline used in fictional stories were not relevant, and by their very nature at the whim of the storyteller. Over the millennia, re-tellers of the stories frequently added details, and characters that were often inconsistent with the other stories. No one knew and no one cared, as they were mostly just for entertainment.

For the more serious devotees, these stories were the basis for a religion, and many aspects of the stories were used to focus worshippers' attention, and they were therefore treated by many at the time as historical facts. They focused their attention on those gods and goddesses that were consistent with their beliefs and values.

The best example that I can use to demonstrate the challenge of chronology, is referencing a main character known as Pandora. As she is the first human woman, she features in her own story, but she was created by Hephaestus, the son of Zeus and Hera, and it happened when Zeus and Hera were already married. But Zeus met and fell in love with Europa, a human woman, who was alive before he married

Hera, and before he had a son to ask to make the first woman. Challenging!

As an author with a particular attention to detail, (at least I believe I do), the chronology of Greek mythological events became increasing important to me as the list of novellas planned for this series grew to thirteen.

I have therefore prepared a simple chronology (that may or may not be consistent with other writers of this genre) to assist readers in sorting out the sequence of events that occur in the stories that I am sharing with you. (Spoiler alert!)

I now believe that Greek Mythology Chronology should be a legitimised field of study all on its own. (Perhaps it already is?)

The novella.	The details of the event.
Pisces	Gaia forms the earth, oceans and skies. She is the earth mother.
Pisces	Gaia gives birth to Uranus.
Pisces	Cronus is born and defeats Uranus when he is released from confinement.
Pisces	Aphrodite is born.
Capricorn	Pricus is the father of the sea-goats.
Pisces	Cronus is crowned king and marries Rea. Zeus is one of their six children.
Centaurus	Cronus mates with Philyra. Chiron is born.
Pandora	Prometheus creates a race of human men - It is known as the golden age.
Pisces	Zeus defeats Cronus and Zeus is crowned King of the Gods.
Pisces	Zeus marries Metis, Athena is born, but Metis dies.

Pandora   Prometheus creates a second race of human men -
               It is known as the silver age.
Pandora   Prometheus creates a third race of human men -
               It is known as the bronze age.
Pisces   Zeus marries but then quickly divorces Themis.
Pandora   Prometheus creates a fourth race of human men -
               It is known as the iron age.
Sagittarius   Crotus invents the bow and arrow.
Pisces   Zeus marries Hera. Ares, Eileithyia,
               Hephaestus, and Hebe are born.
Pisces   Aphrodite arrives at Mount Olympus
               and marries Hephaestus.
Pandora   Hephaestus creates Pandora
               as the first human woman.
Taurus   Zeus meets Europa.
Scorpio   Zeus mates with Leto and
               Apollo and Artemis are born.
Scorpio   Poseidon mates with Euryale and
               Orion is born.
Scorpio   Atalanta is recused as an infant and
               she now runs with Artemis
Aries   Zeus creates a cloud nymph named Nephele.
Aries   Poseidon mates with Theophane and
               Chrysomallos is born.
Aries   Nephele marries Athamas and
               Helle and Phrixus are born.
Aries   Chrysomallos rescues Helle and Phrixus.
Ophiuchus   Apollo mates with Coronis and
               Asclepius is born.
Cancer/Leo   Zeus mates with Alkmene and
               Herakles is born.
Gemini   Zeus mates with Leda and
               Polydeuces and Castor are born.
Pisces   Aphrodite mates with Ares. Eros is born.

Scorpio	Orion meets and befriends Hephaistos.
Virgo/Libra	Zeus visits Themis and Astraea.
Cancer/Leo	Herakles is assigned the first of his ten labours.
Cancer/Leo	Herakles befriends Chiron.
Centaurus	Chiron befriends Herakles.
Gemini	Castor and Polydeuces join the Argo crew
Cancer/Leo	Herakles joins Argo crew.
Gemini	Atalanta asks to join Argo crew.
Scorpio	Orion meets Artemis.
Centaurus	Chiron commences as a teacher.
Gemini	Herakles is inadvertently separated from the Argo.
Cancer/Leo	Herakles resumes his labours.
Scorpio	Orion duels with the giant scorpion.
Gemini	Jason and Argo crew return with the Golden Fleece.
Gemini	Calydonian Boar Hunt.
Gemini	Atalanta joins the Calydonian Boar Hunt
Cancer/Leo	Herakles accidentally wounds Chiron
Centaurus	Chiron makes his plea to Zeus.
Pisces	The Greeks and the Trojans start a war that lasts ten years.
Aquarius	Zeus meets Ganymede.
Cancer/Leo	Herakles becomes immortal and marries Hebe.
Pisces	Atalanta competes in a running race against her potential suitors.
Gemini	Castor and Polydeuces become immortal.
Pisces	Aphrodite an Eros escape Typhon.

1

The story of Virgo and Libra.

Zeus, King of the God's, and therefore the most powerful omnipotent being in the known world had many passions. Most of the gods and goddess of Mount Olympus would declare it to be the pursuit of sexual congress, as it seemed to them that it dominated his lifestyle. But when he was not tormenting, fornicating, drinking, or merry making, he enjoyed morphing into his giant eagle form and flying. As a god, he could just materialize at any destination, but flying to it was more fun. The other birds of prey gave him open skies, and he rarely encountered any problems on his travels. His arrivals were planned to be unobtrusive and guarded, and he always circled his destination to give him time to evaluate the prevailing conditions. Today, he was flying to a group of islands known as Thera.

Recently, he had heard many unsettling reports about what the people of Thera were doing, and he concluded that it was time to visit them and assess the situation for himself.

***

1

The majority of people who live on the islands of Thera are enjoying a time of peace, innocence, and tranquility. They are isolated from the mainland and they have few visitors, other than the Hellas (Greeks), Mycenaean, Hittites, Egyptian, and Phoenicians, who were seafaring merchants that sailed to Thera to do business. These seafaring traders regularly visited the islanders, and they brought with them livestock, timber, and metal ingots to trade for the islanders produce which included preserved seafood, textiles, pottery, pumice, and saffron. Trade, whilst significant, does not dominate the islander's lives.

The Theran's have advanced at a faster rate to the other Greek peoples, as they were unencumbered by their less progressive traditions, rules, and customs. They are also far away from the hectic lives of the gods and goddesses who work and play at Mount Olympus, yet they are still under these God's influences. Fortunately for the islanders, the goddesses that live and work with them are progressive and inclusive. They are using the Theran's to develop a model society, which they planned to introduce into mainstream humanity, but only when they have proven that it will work.

The Theran group of islands are situated in the southern part of the Aegean Sea, about halfway between the Greek mainland and Hittite empire (now known as Türkiye). Their capital is a large town that the people named Akrotiri, after the promontory on which it is located. There are just over seven thousand inhabitants calling Akrotiri home, and about another three thousand people who live among the scattered remote villages and other hamlets that are now firmly established across the island group.

Four goddesses chose to live permanently on their islands with them. They were trusted and respected, and the people felt more that they were one of them, rather than being representatives of Mount Olympus. The exuded the qualities of beauty, intelligence, and a prevailing sense of goodwill to others.

Themis is their matriarch. She was the oldest and the most experienced of all of them. She is a Titan daughter of Gaia, our earth mother, and she is also the sister of Cronus, Zeus's father, and therefore she is Zeus's aunt. Though capable with a sword, she managed to avoid the Titanomachy and kept out of harm's way during the Titan's and Gods struggle for dominion. In this way she avoided both Zeus's wrath, and the internment that the other warfaring titans suffered after they were defeated.

She later became Zeus's second wife, and though they loved and respected each other, they did not actually enjoy being married to each other. They both acknowledged that their sexual intimacy was fantastic, but they eventually agreed that enjoying great sex was not a sufficiently strong enough reason to keep them in any type of binding relationship. There reunions however, were often consummated with an impromptu, uninhibited, yet somewhat discreet copulation.

Previously, when Themis lived at Mount Olympus, she took the infant Apollo under her care and she guided him during his formative years. At the time she was the goddess of wisdom and good counsel, and she was often sought out as an Oracle. Her temple, where she received petitioners was located at Mount Parnassus. She later passed on her gift of prophecy and the responsibility of helping people with their divination's to Apollo when he came of age.

Now, her current tasks involve the administration of equity and balance within the community. She was capable of restoring order after the chaos. She would reason with the complainants, and they all readily accepted her judgements, as they kept the peace and allowed the plaintiff to get fair compensation for their losses incurred by an erroneous defendant. With her logic and reasoning she brought about justice and balance. Her values and methods were highly respected and often emulated.

Themis always exhibits a high standard of moral values. She never succumbs to Dionysus charm or influence. Other than Zeus, she has little need for relationships and she remained unmarried after she and Zeus had divorced. Together they have three daughters who are named Dike, the goddess of justice, Eunomia, the goddess of law and order, and Eirene, the goddess of peace.

Both Eunomia and Eirene have travelled extensively. Eunomia dispenses good order and governance according to the equitable laws of Zeus's kingdom. Eirene, as the goddess of peace remind the people of the harmony and prosperity that everyone enjoys during the peaceful times. She cannot prevent a war, or even intercede in any rising conflict, but she does remind people of the benefits of peace and security, and in this way, she encourages them to compromise, as opposed to them engaging in hostilities. Though Eunomia and Eirene are currently estranged from their mother, Themis is exceptionally proud of all of her daughters.

Dike however, chose to live on the island with her mother. Zeus has acknowledged her as his daughter, but he contributed nothing in the way of her parenting. This did not impinge Dike's development as she thrived living and working with her mother. Dike assisted Themis by being the goddess of the execution of judgements. Her role is to ensure that the parties involved did what they were instructed to do after an official verdict was pronounced. If they failed, then she prosecutes that person to fulfill their obligations, and then punish them proportionately to their crime. In her way, Dike was an enforcer, and for this reason she was both feared and respected.

Another goddess that calls the islands home, is Nemesis. She is the goddess of wrathful retribution, and in particular she intercedes when humans exhibited excessive pride, or a destabilising over confidence. She acts kindly toward decent people, and she spends much of her time ensuring the equitable sharing of the available resources. In this way she is trusted by the majority of people who respect her fairness. However, any people who believed they deserved more, without supporting evidence, will suffer from her punishment. Nemesis does have a sense of humour, but she hides it well. She is often called away from the island to investigate an alleged crime, and she determines the penalty for the guilty. She is symbolic of the retribution that the perpetrators can expect when planning a crime. For many people, she is an effective deterrent.

Lastly, there is Astraea. She is the daughter of Astraeus and Eos. She is principally known as the virgin goddess, and she exhibits qualities of justice, purity, and precision. Her vow of celibacy is respected, but it has also made her a popular topic of conversation throughout Zeus's kingdom. There are some males who fear that her vows of chastity will become more popular among other females. Significantly, Artemis and Atalanta had also declared their sexual abstinence.

Astraea is the goddess that criminals fear the most. When they come to her attention, their crimes are thoroughly investigated, and when they are proven guilty, they are punished according to their crime. Unlike Themis, who seeks to restore balance between plaintiffs, Astraea seeks either an enforced subjugation, or a penalty. These penalties ranged from punishments such as a forfeiture of their valuables, or performing a servitude to the community as a way of redeeming themselves for their crimes. If they were deemed a risk of re-offending, then their punishment is incarceration, or even banishment. Astraea describes their wrongdoings as crimes against society, and her measured retributions are deemed a persuasive method of dissuading others from undertaking criminal activities. Without her punishments, there would be no consequences for criminals for any of their wrongdoings.

Her father, Astraeus is an astrological deity, and he personified the starry night sky. Their names are forever associated with the appearance of the stars at nighttime, and it is likely that the terms astronomy and astrology are derived from them. Astraea's name means "star maiden".

Eos is Astraeus's wife, and Astraea's mother, and she personifies the dawn. They live near the great river Oceanus, and when Eos awakens, she allows the sunshine of Helios to shine on the lands once more, turning the night into day. Astraea has four brothers, known as the Anemoi, and they are the gods of the four winds.

Astraea also chose to work on the island with Themis, Dike, and Nemesis, to learn how to better assist in developing their humans into a modern, cultured, and uniquely civilized society. She hopes that they will become the standard for all future human behaviour. Some of the gods think she is an idealist, but she strongly believes in punishing criminals and in maintaining good order for the majority of the people who both want it, and deserved it.

For the people of Thera, the prevalence of law and order enacted for them by these four goddesses meant that there is minimal criminal activity on the island. As far as the goddesses were concerned, their teachings and practices of the common law and civil law, performed perfectly in this community. They believe that one day these laws will also work in the wider societies on the mainland. They are agreed that one day they will start teaching these values and laws to all the Greek humans in Zeus's kingdom.

***

A massive ravine divided Akrotiri. On one side of the ravine the ground was ideal for living. There was easy access to an ample supply of clean water. The landscape featured flat fields that were suitable for much of the housing and communal buildings that the majority of the people who lived at Akrotiri needed. Their farms produced abundant food crops, and they also grew fodder for their livestock. There is ample room for children to run and play and for staging communal sporting events. There is a jetty suitable for loading and unloading of the fishing fleet and the visiting merchants, but it was not considered a safe stretch of water to anchor a boat or ship. This jetty could only be used when the tide was high and the seas were exceptionally calm.

On the other side of the ravine was a natural harbour, which was perfect for the fishing fleet, and the pleasure craft that the townspeople enjoyed using. Most of the fishermen and their families preferred living close to their boats. Here, the housing followed the contours of the hills. The ravine that divided the town was deep and narrow. The path leading to its base was cumbersome, as was the climb up the other side, so services to the families that lived near the harbour were limited. It was readily agreed that a well-designed and strongly constructed bridge, was urgently needed.

Previous attempts at bridge building had failed and in the most recent collapse, several people were injured. Themis had a plan for a bridge and she convinced the engineers that her new bridge had to start its span a long way from the edge of the ravine. In this way they would avoid the effects of erosion when heavy rains came. Some of the engineers were sceptical as Themis was a respected arbitrator, but she was not an engineer. The engineers pushed for a long-term solid structure, but Themis argued that a well-made rope bridge would be much quicker to construct, and the fishermen agreed as their need for the bridge was considered urgent, especially for their wives and children.

***

Construction of the rope bridge had started that morning, but progress was stalled when the main block and tackle jammed near the middle. The block and tackle is used to carry materials and people across the void as needed. It would be used to pull over the heavy ropes that would form the walls and floor of the bridge.

A delicate repair operation was now underway, as a brave young man walked precariously out across the ravine balancing on a thick rope that was stretched taut across the divide. He held a long balancing pole in his hands as he nervously crept his way to the middle. There were three other ropes securing him to a leather harness that he wore on his waist. These ropes were slowly being let out by his safety team on one side of the ravine, and were drawn in by the others on the far side. In this way, if he lost his balance and fell, the three safety teams would reduce the speed of his fall, and prevent him from being dashed on the sides of the ravine, and he would then be lowered safely to the bottom.

As he neared the middle of the rope, the man looked about uncertain of what to do with the pole. With one hand on the block and tackle he tried to throw the pole to the edge of the ravine. He wobbled precariously as he did so, but the pole missed the edge and fell noisily to the ground below. As he steadied himself, someone in the crowd shouted out cautions. When he was ready, he looked about to assure his watchers that he was okay by smiling and waving. He gingerly reached up to start work on dislodging the knot in the block and tackle.

The three younger goddesses, Nemesis, Astraea, and Dike, all watched him in fascinated silence. All were fearful that he might fall, and they inadvertently held their breath. Themis also watched the man with some trepidation as she was responsible for him as she supervised and coordinated all the bridge construction activities. All of them had confidence that her plan would work and they had only ever known her to succeed.

Whether the people who were assembled to watch him were there to witness the young man's bravery and skill, or if they wanted to be present to see him fall, was irrelevant. They were witnessing an unusual event, and the size of the crowd was slowly growing larger on each side of the ravine as news of his dangerous task quickly spread.

The bridge was Themis's own design, and she did not want to disappoint her people or herself. It consisted of five main heavy-duty ropes that were made using Jute fibres. These were spun using spinning wheels and then they were woven by skilled rope makers. The finished ropes were soaked in olive oil to strengthen and waterproof them.

Two extra thick ropes would form the upper span of the bridge. They would be held high by securing these ropes to the top of thick vertical poles that had been firmly embedded into the ground. There were two poles on each side of the ravine, one pair on each side of the span. The ropes that would form the top of the bridge were to be held down securely anchored into the ground on a forty-five-degree angle from the top of the pole stretching away from the span. It was also planned that the path leading up to the bridge, and the area immediately surrounding the poles and its supports was going to be paved. In this way the heavy rains would not wash away the soil and therefore weaken the structure.

Suspended from these top ropes, the fastened dropping ropes would be used to hold the two outside floor ropes in place. From them, sturdy planks would be secured to form the walking platform of the bridge itself. A fifth rope would be strung and secured under the middle of the walking platform to increase its strength and stability. Themis believed that when the bridge was finished, it would be able to support the weight of many people, and that it would be strong enough to support a laden cart pulled by a donkey.

Earlier that morning, an archer had successfully loosed an arrow across the ravine. No great feat in itself, however, this arrow trailed a lengthy thin thread. At the receiving end the people had given the arrow plenty of room to land. They retrieved the arrow and pulled on the thread which was attached to an even thicker string and this was subsequently attached to an even stronger rope. It was this rope that was now securely tied taut and properly secured on both sides of the ravine. They attached a block and tackle to it so that it could be pulled from either side of the ravine. This would be used to carry the building materials to the village side of the ravine and be used extensively during the construction of the rope bridge. On one of its traverses, the block and tackle got jammed.

Now, supervised by Themis, the man was carefully balancing on the rope, approaching the knot in the block in order to free it. He reached up and with his free hand he started to loosen the knot. He moved it back and forth until he was satisfied that he had freed it. He smiled at Themis who signalled her encouragement. The crowd cheered.

As he turned to head back his legs began to shake and the rope began to wobble violently. His mother cried out to be careful. The young man turned to glance at her as his legs gave way. He scrambled for the rope with his hands, but his own weight was too much for him, and he was unable to steady himself and he fell off.

As he plummeted, one of the safety crews lost their grip on the support rope, and his body now arced toward the ravine's walls where he would be dashed against the rocks and then continue to fall to his certain death. Just at that same moment, a giant eagle swooped down from the sky, seemingly materializing out of nowhere and it caught the man seconds before impact. The eagle had skillfully managed to grasped the man's arms without injury him and it slowly ascended. The eagle deposited the frightened young man beside Themis, and he fell to the ground weeping from both relief and fright. With a deafening screech, the eagle flapped its mighty wings, rose back into the sky and turned and headed in the direction of the goddess's home.

Themis checked on the man's condition. When she was satisfied that he was okay, she smiled and waved to the crowd yelling 'He is fine.'

The crowd cheered and applauded as the young man released himself from the safety ropes and re-joined his mother. Together, they melded into the crowd.

'We will stop work and resume early tomorrow morning,' she advised her bridge construction management team. They nodded their appreciation, as they also had enough excitement for one day.

Themis turned to the three other goddesses. 'We have a visitor.'

***

In earlier times, the Theran's were regarded as part of the Minoan culture, but their association with mainland Greece meant that their culture was shifting away from Minoan ways, and they were becoming more like the Mycenaeans and Greeks. They were fortunate to be unaffected by the ongoing struggle between the Greeks and the Mycenaeans, whose homes had to be protected by massive fortresses due to the ongoing threat of invasion. On Thera, there are no fortresses or even fortifications, as they are not required.

There is an ample supply of food and fresh water, and the islanders efficiently manage their farms so there are never any food shortages.

The residents look out for each other, and there is a prevailing sense of community. The people enjoy life with their families and friends. They laugh often and are genuinely happy. They co-operate and flourish as a human population, and their needs and wants are simple and easily satisfied.

The tranquil blue waters that surround the island are abundant with fish and other marine life, and the sea provides much of the diet for the Theran's. Many of its inhabitants are involved in the fishing, gathering, preparation, and preserving this highly valued resource.

***

The four goddesses live in a modern expansive hill top mansion that overlooked both sides of the ravine. The view on the northern side was of the suburbs of Akrotiri. On the other side it overlooked the harbour and the fishermen's homes. On the western side of the home they enjoyed expansive views of the Mediterranean Sea which stretched out before them. To the east was the main body of the island of Thera which was used for farming and still had significant areas of natural vegetation.

They each had their own bed chambers and private retreats, and they shared a communal kitchen, meals, and lounge area.

'It was fortunate that I happened to be flying overhead,' Zeus told everyone as they entered the main hall.

Zeus had made himself comfortable on a couch. He had located wine and a cup, and had helped himself while he waited for the others to return.

'It is good to see you again, Zeus,' Themis told him. 'Thank you for your help.'

'I have been away too long,' he replied. Looking at her he added. 'I have missed you.' He stood up, placed his cup on a table and walked up to Themis to properly embrace her.

Themis laughed.

Zeus tried to appear hurt. 'Why do you laugh at me?' he asked.

'With your growing list of consorts, I doubt it very much that you would ever miss anyone.'

'It is true. I am an exceptionally busy god,' he agreed. 'Just ask Hera,' he laughed.

'Your reputation always precedes you.'

Zeus the stared at the three other women. 'That one on the left. Is she, my daughter?' Zeus asked playfully.

'Hello father,' Dike spoke.

'Dike, you are more beautiful each time I see you,' Zeus complimented.

'Thank you, father,' she responded. 'But it has only been six weeks since you were last here.'

'Too long my dear,' he told her, he then turned and was now looking at Nemesis when he asked. 'How are you, Nemesis?'

'I am well, thank you for asking,' she replied smiling.

'And Astraea,' Zeus examined her up and down.

'Yes, my lord,' she replied respectfully.

'I wish you would look upon me, as your father,' he told her.

'I would be honoured, my lord.' she responded. But my father Astraeus watches over me every night. He may get jealous of our relationship.'

'I believe that Astraeus has neglected you since you announced that you do not want to join him as a star goddess. You are aware that your predilection for involving yourself in human activities disappoints him, and so he has not been much of a father to you, has he?' he asked rhetorically.

'No,' Astraea said softly her face portraying her sadness as she agreed.

'Then I should adopt you and that will remove all doubt,' he invited her capitulation with a generous smile.

This banter between them had occurred on each of Zeus's visits to Thera. It was Themis's idea that Zeus should become an adoptive father to Astraea. She felt she would have more advantages being regarded in this way. Themis loved all three women as her daughters, and Zeus had so many of them that one more did not present a challenge. Astraea had resisted all previous invitations and so it became a challenge for Zeus to get her to concede. Zeus enjoyed a challenge and he hated to lose.

Astraea smiled. She had already decided to accept his offer of paternity, as any escalation of her rejection of him would become problematic for her role on the island. She also hoped that by being his daughter that more people would respect her vow of celibacy. 'I accept. Thank you, my lord... or should I now call you father?' she asked.

Zeus stared at Themis who nodded.

'Yes, father would do,' he answered her. 'Would you like a formal ceremony?'

'No!,' she replied laughing.

'Fine. That is for the best, as I would not know how to organise one,' he explained as he laughed to himself.

'Good,' she smiled and seemed confused as to what to do. So, she stepped toward him and timidly embraced her newly adopted father.

'Right.' Zeus added, and as he enjoyed a loving embrace, he pulled her closer and gave her a welcoming hug in return.

'Is this why you came to Thera?' Themis asked him when Astraea managed to extricate herself from him. Zeus has a reputation for becoming too familiar with his daughters and granddaughters.

'What..., no,' Zeus appeared flustered.

Themis said nothing. She smiled at him and gave him that look that a woman can give a male when she wants to communicate a taboo to him. She wanted to ensure that Zeus knew that Astraea was out of bounds as a potential sexual conquest.

The way that they stared at each other meant that he understood her clearly. He did not seem disappointed. He broke off with another smile and then he changed and appeared to be serious. 'I am here to check on the progress of your humans. I have received several reports from some of the gods returning to Mount Olympus after holidaying or working here. I came to see them for myself.'

'What would you like to know about them?' she asked. 'You have not shown much interest in them before.'

'That is true. Perhaps we could talk more about this with a spread of food before us, and another cup of wine in our hand,' he suggested.

'Are you tired and hungry father?' Astraea asked him.

'We are gods my dear. We do not get tired, or hungry. But I will admit that I do enjoy eating tasty foods, drinking quality wines, and then sleeping. All in that order,' he smiled.

'Then we will feast on local delicacies, and drink local wine, as the four of us will explain to you about what has been happening on our little island,' Themis suggested. She knew from experience that feeding Zeus his favourite savouries was the best way to relax him, and that was the way to make him more amiable.

'Fantastic,' Zeus was evidently delighted. 'I find that wine not only elevates my thinking, but it also makes me appear more intellectual to others. Please lead on,' he invited with a gesture of his hand.

The four women led Zeus to the temple dining area. There they were greeted by Themis's palace staff who attended to them with washing bowls and towels. Fires were lit for warmth and light.

Roasted meats, cooked vegetables, and fresh fruits were served on a low table surrounded by massive comfortable cushions. Several amphorae of wine were within easy reach and one had already been used to pour wine into large ornately carved marble drinking cups. Zeus smiled and was clearly pleased with the offering. They arranged themselves around the banquet and selected what food to put into their bowls and then sat down and started eating.

'How many humans do you have living here on Thera?' he asked between mouthfuls.

'There are just over ten thousand people living on the islands,' Nemesis informed him.

They participate in many trades and developed many skills,' added Themis.

'I hear from the gods and goddess who have frequented here, that the people are doing well,' Zeus added.

The women were silent, but they smiled, clearly pleased with Zeus's assessment as if reflected well of their efforts to enhance the humans under their care and nurturing.

'And how many of the gods are currently on the island?' Zeus asked as he smiled.

At any one time there may be twenty or so,' Themis replied. "I do not know how many there are here today, but I could easily find out for you,' she offered.

'You don't keep a track on them?' Zeus asked.

'There is no need. It seems that we are a popular destination. Some come for inspiration, others to relax. Some, like us, come to Thera to experiment with new ideas and improved ways of doing things. Do you want me to summons those currently on the island for a meeting?'

'Not yet,' Zeus responded. 'Who is here?'

'Your sister, Demeter,' explained Themis.

'She will be planting wheat crops, I suppose,' speculated Zeus. 'Is her friend Eunostus with her?'

'No, but Hestia is here,' added Astraea.

'Nothing beats eating fresh bread that is still warm from the oven,' Zeus mused.

'Ploutos,' contributed Nemesis.

'Ploutos? Which one is he?' Zeus asked, confused.

'Demeter's son,' Themis explained.

'I think I forgot that Demeter had a son,' Zeus added feigning innocence.

'He is your nephew!' exclaimed Dike.

'We are a large family... It is difficult to keep track of us all. What does Ploutos do again?' he asked appearing confused.

'Ploutos attends to man's wealth creation through agricultural pursuits,' Nemesis explained.

'That is one of the things I want to investigate,' Zeus was becoming increasingly interested.

'Plus, it seems he has desires for our Astraea!' she added.

'Oh, stop it!' Astraea rebuked her. She was smiling, but she tried to look annoyed at Nemesis.

'He is charming and exceptionally handsome,' Nemesis continued.

'And strong, and kind, and intelligent,' Themis added, smiling at Astraea.

'I am sure that Astraea has many suitors,' Zeus concluded.

'She certainly does,' Nemesis confirmed. 'But no nibbles as yet, as she claims she remains resolutely disinterested in men,' she added.

'Father is not here to learn about my love life,' Astraea assured them.

'You need to have one to be able to talk about it,' chided Dike.

'Later,' Themis cautioned them all. Ploutos has encouraged farmers to increase their wealth by selling their surplus harvest to the merchant traders. It has caused some issues as now the local islanders have to pay more and match the traders' rates to keep the food here.'

'Ploutos has convinced some of the smaller farmers to give their land to the bigger farmers and have them specialise in profitable crops in exchange for a larger share of the profits. Trading and exporting are two significant growth industries,' Dike explained.

'Before that, they all just shared everything!' Astraea declared. 'Life was so much simpler. I fear our golden age of tranquility is being replaced by the greedy pursuit of profits.'

'I am curious about this wealth creation. This is a relatively new concept for humans and I hoped that it would not happen this soon,' Zeus told them.

'I never saw the need for it,' Themis commented.

'As god's, wealth is abstract concept. We get what we desire, so accumulating anything beyond experiences is redundant.'

'Is wealth creation a bad thing?' Dike asked.

'It is a change in their behaviour. Up to now, humans mostly increase their wealth by conquest or by accumulation, or through the sale of manufactured items. It never actually amounted to much. Now that it seems your humans are initiating the start of becoming wealth hoarders. We need to discuss these changes of these human's behaviour.'

'But surely, these types of changes must be happening everywhere?' Themis asked, confused at Zeus's concern.

So far, they are only occurring here on Thera,' Zeus answered. 'Elsewhere, human progress is still happening at a much slower pace. Because of our interference, Thera is rapidly becoming an advanced civilization, and we must discuss what effect this will have here and on neighbouring societies. It will have consequences, as it will ultimately have a negative impact on how humans behave towards us gods.' He paused but then continued with his warning. 'Any independent thinking on their part will eventually interfere with how committed they are to worshipping us.'

The women said nothing. They stared at each other with some embarrassment as they were realised that Zeus was including them as part of the problem.

'The four of you are living permanently with your humans, so perhaps you are too close to the changes, and so you do not see or understand the risks that you are taking. In the morning, I would want to hear a report from each of you. I want to learn what it is that you do with the humans, and what impact the four of you are having on their development. Tomorrow, I want to meet with some of your key humans, and then later we will meet again to talk some more.'

'It is not just us...' Themis defended.

'I understand that. I also want learn what effect the visits from other gods are having on your humans. These changes like "wealth creation," concern me.'

The women still did not speak.

'I would especially want to see first-hand the new things that are happening in the day to day lives of the people of Thera,' Zeus affirmed. 'If that is okay with all of you?'

'Yes, Zeus, of course it is,' Themis replied as she accepted for the four of them. She was now becoming concerned that Zeus was now somehow planning to either impede or reverse the progress of all that they had accomplished on Thera.

'Now, I am tired. There was a strong head wind pushing against me. Flying here was more challenging than normal. I think I must have upset Eurus at some time, as he ignored my commands to desist.' Eurus is the god of the east wind, and he has a reputation for being irascible and retributive.

'Maybe, he did not want you to visit us,' Astraea speculated coyly.

'Humph,' Zeus dismissed her. Eurus was an influential god, but not with Zeus. 'I know that he is your brother, and he might think that he is being protective. I might think that he was attempting to dissuade me from visiting here. But I also know that is not true, as I am welcomed everywhere.'

'Well, I am glad you came to visit us, father,' Astraea said graciously as she stood up. 'I'm tired and I am going to bed. Sleep well,' she offered the others as she exited the room.

'Me too, my wings needed a stretch, but the flying has made me tired. It was a long flight,' Zeus stretched and yawned.

Nemesis and Dike picked up on their cue to leave the room. They both stood up and walked toward the exit. 'But still, flying is quicker than walking,' Nemesis joked and was smiling. She waved her goodnight and they headed for their bedchambers.

'Especially over water,' Dike contributed as she followed Nemesis.

'There is that,' Zeus agreed.

They laughed.

Themis and Zeus sat close together in silence. Zeus then turned to her and spoke gently. 'I do desire you as my bed companion.' Zeus turned to his ex-wife. 'Themis, my darling, can I tempt you?'

'Possibly,' she replied with a mischievous grin. They often copulated on his visits. 'I was worried that perhaps you were too tired? Can I hope that you can keep up with me?' she challenged.

'Of course,' Zeus laughed. 'Why would you ever doubt me?'

'Well, you do fall seem to fall asleep so easily these days,' she teased.

They both laughed again and then kissed passionately.

***

Astraea, Dike, and Nemesis entered their anteroom. The room adjoined their sleeping quarters and it was furnished with comfortable chairs and decorated with frescos depicting day to day activities of the humans. The women used it for impromptu meetings and discussions as it had a congenial atmosphere and a sunny disposition with views overlooking the harbour.

They started their discussions in earnest.

'Astraea, you surprised me!' Dike said as she walked up to her and gave her a congratulatory hug.

'By me finally accepting father's invitation to adopt me?'

'Wow, yes, now we are officially sisters!' Dike added.

'I do wish that my real parents were involved in my life,' lamented Astraea. 'I have often felt like I was an orphan.'

'What does it matter?' Nemesis asked her.

'Themis has always been a mother to me, and the two of you have been my sisters since, well it seems like forever. But it would be nice to know for sure if my actual parents care about me,' she said and then paused. She drew in a deep breath and continued. 'When I travel to Mount Olympus I always get asked by some idiotic god, "so, is Zeus your father?" and I am sick of it.' She paused to take in a deep breath.

'So, Zeus wants me to be his daughter, and he respects me, so I decided that I might as well accept his offer and make it legitimate.'

'That would have been Dionysus, I expect,' Nemesis. 'When he learns that you are Zeus's daughter then he will stop trying to get you inebriated and desist from pestering you for coitus.'

'He has tried to do both those things with me, despite my proclamations of sexual abstinence.'

'And Iacchus?' asked Dike.

'He is more of a pest than Dionysus,' Astraea explained. 'He once revealed his engorged genitalia to me with an invitation to "Go riding." Astraea then stood up pulled her skirt aside and motioned how Iacchus waved his member about the room.

Dike and Nemesis burst out in laughter.

After they settled Dike continued. 'Calyce is no help.'

'She is as often as drunk as the rest of them.'

'All women should help each other.'

'That woman does not even help herself...' Astraea paused in thought. 'Well not often enough.'

'I can see why you avoid going to Mount Olympus,' agreed Dike.

'Why do you go?' asked Astraea.

'I enjoy visiting my other sisters, Eunomia and Eirene. They do not travel to Thera anymore, since their argument with mother.'

The mood became solemn and they sat in silence for a while. Astraea interrupted their melancholy. 'I am the daughter of Astraeus and Eos,' she explained. 'But that in itself does not make any sense.'

'How come?'

'Well, my father is the god of dusk and my mother is the goddess of the dawn! How did they ever get to meet to... you know?'

'They would have had enough time during dusk and dawn to make a baby,' explained Dike. It does not take much time. But their loving cuddle after coitus would not have lasted very long,' she advised grinning sheepishly.

'I suppose. I never properly thought that through, did I?' she laughed at herself. 'Being a committed virgin does limit my understanding of such things.'

The others laughed politely with her.

'Have you ever asked them?' asked Dike.

'I did once,' she told them. 'They asked "Why does it matter? After all, Themis is caring for you".'

Dike and Nemesis did not reply.

'So, after a while it felt like it did not actually matter at all,' she added.

'Themis is a fantastic mother, and she has loved you like a daughter since I can remember,' offered Dike.

Dike then added, 'The four of us are bound by the truth, justice, and fairness.'

'And balance.'

'And righteous indignation,' contributed Nemesis.

'That is yours alone,' said Astraea.

'No, it is not. We all hate injustice.'

They sat in silence, letting their words soak in. Slowly they rose and entered their respective bed chambers. Their rooms were large and each had large beds with dressing robes and a washing basin. These three women were generally inseparable, and they frequently met with each other for impromptu meetings, and to give each other assistance. They most often ate together in the dining room and between them, they had few secrets.

Themis had her own bed chamber on the other side of the palace as she preferred to work alone. They would often meet and discuss issues with her. The three younger women had readily accepted their role of learning under Themis tutorlidge . Fortunately for the people of Thera, it had worked out well.

The people were mostly respectful and law abiding. They were productive and delighted in acquiring new skill and inventing new and better ways of doing things.

The island also had a solid reputation with the gods and goddesses of Mount Olympus as a progressive society and so many Gods and Goddesses visited the island to encourage their development and to try out new ideas with these enlightened humans.

***

The islanders were for the most part self-sufficient. Timber for construction was scarce and so most of the dwellings were made of rammed earth. Their housing engineers were skilled at utilising the terrain to full advantage, and so many of the homes hugged the contours of the steep hills that feature prominently across the main island. The outer walls and roofs were lined with materials sourced from ancient volcanic eruptions known as ejecta, as they provided excellent insulation from the elements.

The engineers also developed a complex plumbing system, delivering both hot and cold water through separate pipes directly into many homes. The hot water emanated from hot water springs from a geothermic source. The fresh water came from catchments higher in the hills, that were contoured to capture the frequent rains. Their drainage system was also sophisticated and so human waste was efficiently flushed away from the habitats, and therefore the town had a clean smell about it.

Their main activities were producing high quality metal art, textile weaving, and pottery. The artisans were respected and many families enjoyed having private frescoes decorating their homes. The artists used water-based pigments to paint art that described everyday life on the island. Frescos depicted scenes of fishing, merchant vessels with visiting traders, pottery, domestic life, sport, outdoor landscapes, and wildlife. They were painted directly on to the fine plaster walls that were constructed over rough plaster and a wall of straw. These walls were designed to breathe so that any dampness would not affect the paintings. Using these technique was their way to ensure that they would be long lasting. There was also an abundance of public art that depicted scenes of community, leisure, and prosperity.

They were successful in agriculture and their crop yields were impressive. They were able to efficiently bring the water to their crops, and farmers were skilled in soil improvement, weed and pest control, and crop rotation. The goddess Demeter spent much of her time with the farmers on Thera, and they benefited greatly from her wisdom and kind ways of teaching them the most efficient methods of farming and crop management. One crop that performed particularly well was the crocus plants. They grew saffron stamens that the women harvested. Saffron featured prominently in the local cuisine, and the surplus crop was a valuable export commodity as it was eagerly sought after by the people of the mainland.

Demeter was one of the few goddesses that was depicted in local art. She was honoured for her contribution to the crop's successes, in particular to the production of saffron.

Theran's made time for their friends and families. They loved to swim, play, and educate their children. They were healthy, kind, playful, and nurturing. For the vast majority of its inhabitants, life on Thera was idyllic.

The people were comfortable with the Gods and Goddesses of Mount Olympus who were frequently visiting them, and they often took guidance and direction from them.

***

The following morning the three women met for breakfast. They each sat on their normal chairs and they contemplated the day's activities while they ate their oats and fruits which were prepared for them by the household kitchen staff.

'What do we need to do to prepare for Zeus's tour?' asked Dike.

'How do we prepare?' asked Astraea.

'What do we say to someone like Zeus? He seems to know every-thing all the time anyway,' Nemesis added.

'His omnipotence and omnipresence are exasperating,' agreed Dike.

'Perhaps we should consult with Themis before we start his in-spection tour,' lamented Astraea.

'I would not want to interrupt her just now,' Dike cautioned. 'I think our mother was a bit busy with father last night!'

They laughed.

'Why are you still a virgin, Astraea?' asked Dike.

'Because it is what I have decided is best for me,' she replied. She was not angry or upset with them. She just explained her resolve calmly and conversationally for the umpteenth time. 'My body, my choice.'

'You do not want to talk about it do you?' Dike continued.

'Not especially,' she paused. 'I am aware that the two of you enjoy doing it.'

'It is called sex,' offered Dike.

'I know what it is called,' she sighed.

'You could try it with, Ploutos?' suggested Nemesis. 'Just to feel what it is like.'

'You will never appreciate what you are missing, if you do not try experiencing sex at least once,' added Dike.

'There are so few of us virgin goddesses. I can think of Artemis, Atalanta, and myself. I happen to prefer being one of them. At least I have their moral support,' she rebuffed.

'And you have ours, it is just that we would like you to understand that you do not have to do it with a man if you do not like them. Sex with a woman can be just as satisfying, if not better,' Dike explained.

Nemesis blushed slightly. She and Dike had a sexual rendezvous the previous night.

'I know you have tried both,' she said wearily. This conversation was becoming tiresome.

'Yes, and as much as I prefer sex with women than with men, it was a man that made me pregnant,' she announced.

'Pregnant!' Dike and Astraea both exclaimed.

'Yes, I am about six weeks I figure,' she told them.

'Wow,' exclaimed Dike.

'Err... who?' asked Astraea.

'It was Zeus,' she replied.

'Zeus our father,' stated Astraea.

'Well, he wouldn't be the first father to impregnate up his own daughter,' Dike offered. 'Alkmene is his granddaughter and that did not stop him.'

They all nodded knowingly. Zeus's tryst with Alkmene produced Herakles, their greatest and most respected hero.

'Does he know?' asked Dike.

'He does not and nor would he care,' explained Nemesis. 'I have not yet told Themis, and I hope that she will be happy for me.'

The three women sat in quiet contemplation.

'I have news to share also,' Dike announced softly.

'What is it?' asked Nemesis.

They looked at her.

'I also had sex with Zeus,' she told them.

'Let me guess.' Astraea uttered contemptuously. 'Six weeks ago?'

'Yes,' Dike replied meekly. 'But I am not pregnant,' she smiled enjoying the anticipation in their eyes.

Nemesis stood up to embrace her. Dike responded by also standing and they held each other tight.

Astraea did nothing. She examined the food and selected a piece of fruit which she ate in stony silence.

'I am pleased and just a little bit scared for you, Nemesis,' declared Dike.

'I am fortunate. Both my sisters will become wonderful aunties,' added Nemesis.

'I vow to remain your loyal and loving maiden sister, and I promise to be a loving and devoted aunt to your baby,' proclaimed Astraea with a half-smile.

They moved toward her and were now sitting on either side of her at the table. They leaned forward and had a group hug.

'I do have one question,' Astraea told them as they broke free from the embrace. 'And I hope it does not sound perverse or intrusive as I would hate for you to think I was interfering on your personal space. I mean, I do not want to sound judgemental.'

They both laughed and continued looking at her expectantly.

'Was it together... at the same... time?'

'Us with Zeus? Ah, no,' answered Dike.

'But it may have been on the same night,' added Nemesis.

'I hope he does not expect anything like that from me,' lamented Astraea.

'No!' they exclaimed jointly.

'He is not like that,' defended Nemesis.

'We will have to make more time to talk about sex and parenting after our meeting with Zeus,' Astraea suggested.

The other two nodded their agreement.

***

After breakfast they freshened up and then they all met in the main chamber. The three young women were now dressed in their day clothes and they had been speculating on the day's activities when Themis and Zeus entered the room.

Themis was glowing. Both Dike and Nemesis recognised the signs and understood the cause.

'I have news,' she told them.

They stared at her and Zeus with anticipation.

'I am pregnant!' Themis declared.

'Since when?' Astraea paused to consider. 'How can you know for sure?' she paused again, and then quickly added 'Is it because of what you did last night? How can you know so soon?' she demanded.

Themis chuckled. Your father has powerful seed. I can already feel movement,' she explained as she rubbed her abdomen.

Dike and Nemesis looked at each other and then rushed to hug Themis.

'Mother! We also have news,' Dike told her excitedly when they broke free.

'What is it,' she demanded.

'Nemesis is pregnant also.'

They screeched in delight and then the four women turned and looked at Zeus.

Zeus said nothing.

'Well, that is exciting news. How far along are you?' asked Themis.

'I am at about six weeks,' Nemesis explained.

'Dike?'

Dike shook her head. They all turned and looked at Zeus again, but he still did not speak.

'And you Astraea?' Themis asked looking at the young woman, but she already knew her response.

'Virginity intact, thank you for caring,' she told them. 'With no plans to change my status.'

Zeus piled food onto a large plate and then sat on a large wooden chair at the table. He was peckish and so he ate with gusto as he motioned the women to join him. They sat and served themselves a drink. He remained quiet while watching them. After a time, he washed down his meal with swig of water. Zeus cleared his throat to explain. 'In regards to the news of your pregnancy, I would just want to say that I am pleased for you both. Naturally, I will contribute my usual support for both of you during your pregnancies, and that will continue after your babies are born.'

They all laughed politely. Zeus had a legendary reputation for contributing nothing.

'How many children have you procreated, father?' Astraea challenged.

'More than I can ever remember, but not as many as I have yet to sire. My seed is strong and my energies for copulation remain boundless. Besides, the more babies I make, the stronger our bloodline, and the more robust our control remains over our human worshipers. Human populations keep expanding as they reproduce at much the same rate as rabbits do. Every time I visit a town or a settlement, there numbers have grown. Humans need us to keep them in check. Our ranks of Gods and Goddesses are stretched thin, and so the babies I make will quickly grow into functioning members of Mount Olympus, and they will work to keep all humans loyal, obedient, and under our control.'

He paused and studied them seriously before continuing. 'Also, all humans love to hear stories about my philandering ways, it gives them something to gossip about over the dinner table. I am a distraction them for them from their personal hardships. You see, I am actually performing a service for them in the form of titillating entertainment.'

They all laughed politely. Zeus did have a legendary reputation for bedding many women, and they all knew that both he and his brother Poseidon's exploits were the hot topics for many people.

Zeus was impatient to start to first stage of his inquiry into the affairs of the Gods involvement with the island's inhabitants.

'Themis. Why don't you start by explaining your role on the island? Please, enlighten me,' he invited.

Themis rose and the others settled back to listen. How she handled her presentation was going to be the format for each of them. They watched and listened with a modicum amount of trepidation.

'Zeus,' she started. 'You have known me for a long time. We have made many children together.'

They all laughed politely.

'I will do as you requested and all I ask of you in return, is that when we have completed the detailed account of our dealing with humans, that you explain what your concerns are to us.'

Zeus nodded his agreement. 'That is fair.'

Themis nodded and smiled. 'My main role is to act as a judge on matters concerning human disagreements. When there is a conflict between them, I ask those affected to present their complaint to me. I ask them for all of the details to determine the facts as much is possible. I allow them to bring in corroborating witnesses to add detail and plausibility to each person's argument. I then think on what I have heard, and their unique circumstances for the predicament that they are in. I then deliberate, reach a decision, and I then deliver a binding judgement,' she explained and then paused to catch her breath. 'My goal is to restore, as much as is possible, the position of the parties before the wrong doings occurred.'

Zeus nodded and motioned for her to continue.

'I am available for counsel for when an individual, or a couple, are troubled. They explain to me their problems and I offer a range of possible solutions that they may or may not choose to use. These are never binding. If, however, their troubles involve errors or conflicts with another person, then then I may choose to bring the defaulters to justice.'

'Much of my counselling is for the benefit of couples and it is often about how they treat each other. I have a special interest in domestic harmony. Many people do not understand their rights under law. Some men do not know how to properly treat their wives, or understand or abide by what rights their wives do have. I help all of them learn and understand their rights, and I help them apply them to their situation,' she said smiling.

'Often my role is to determine what is wrong, who committed the wrong doing, and what must be done to put it right. I seek a balance between conflicting people or groups.'

'What if the wrong doing is intentional and bodily harm is enacted,' Zeus asked. 'How do you punish the guilty individual?'

'Some crimes are punishable by simple restitution, others by forfeiture of wealth, some by community service, and for the severe crimes they are punished by enduring some physical pain.'

'Beatings?'

'More like lashes. But not so much that they need extensive medical treatment. That only adds to the problem. Their pain and recovery act as a powerful deterrent against criminal re-occurrence.' She looked at the others for support. 'We would also want to believe that public punishments serve as an example of the consequences of serious misdeeds.'

'How about incarceration?' Asked Zeus.

'No,' replied Themis. 'It serves no real purpose and others are required to supervise them. Imprisonment also imprisons the jailer.'

'Banishment?'

'That just moves the problem elsewhere, but in certain circumstances we do use it.'

'Bonded servitude or slavery?'

'No. We would prefer not to have slaves on Thera. We do have some and they are treated well. We find that supervised community service seems to be the most appropriate form of punishment. The populace gets something positive out of the incident. I try to direct their labours towards a victim's benefit. This seems to encourage remorse by the guilty, and so they are less likely to reoffend.'

'Execution?'

'Only as an ultimate last resort,' Themis explained. Sentences are enacted quickly and preferably by a member of the injured family. There is no further retribution. We do not believe that crimes are inherited by the other family members of those involved. We only punish those that are proven guilty beyond all doubt.'

'Thank you, Themis,' he motioned to her to return to her seat.

'Astraea, would you go next please?' Zeus invited her to rise and speak.

Astraea looked about the room nervously.

'Yes father.'

She rose and stepped to the place where Themis had done her presentation.

'I am justice. Like Themis, I seek to bring about good order in the activities of all the humans,' she smiled at Themis. 'I work on the premise that a person is innocent until the facts of their misdeeds are proven. In this way people get a fair unbiased opportunity to state their position when another lays a blame of a crime or a misdeed upon them.'

She paused examining Zeus for some reaction, but he sat in silence. Zeus's stoic face betrayed neither approval or issue.

Astraea decided to continue. 'I believe that sometimes individuals are at risk of being blamed unjustly, or they are falsely accused. It can be from the result of an error in understanding of the facts, or through a deception designed to make an innocent person appear guilty, when in reality they are doing it to hide the real perpetrators actions. I work diligently to prevent injustice so that true fairness and equity can prevail.'

She moved to return to her seat.

Zeus stopped her. 'Wait. I have questions.'

Astraea stopped and faced him.

'How can you be certain that the person claiming to be deceived is not the one trying to deceive you?'

She drew in a deep breath before she explained. 'We cross reference the stories of the affected people, and we ask for witnesses to come forth to tell us what they know. We then discuss the case between ourselves before we make a determination.'

'Have you ever subsequently realised that you passed the wrong judgement?' Zeus asked.

'Not to my knowledge,' she looked at Themis for reassurance. And she nodded and smiled her agreement.

'What are the consequences to the guilty?'

'The same as what Themis explained. Restitution, forfeiture of wealth or possessions, work orders, physical pain, and for truly serious cases, death.

'Do you ever act as prosecutor?'

'I often do. When I believe the evidence supports a guilty verdict, I pursue it. No one is above the law or exempt from the penalty of a crime...'

'Thank you, Astraea, you may sit.'

Astraea drew in a deep breath. She nodded gratefully and returned to her chair.

'Dike,' he said as he looked at her. 'Would you please tell me about your role and a bit about what you do?'

'Yes father,' she replied.

Dike rose and also stood where her mother had done her presentation. She cleared her throat and started. 'I am the goddess of moral justice,' she explained. 'I preserve the ways of all men and women, and I determine what is fair and right by law, precedent, tradition, and custom.'

'I also assist mother in her deliberations.' She too looked at Themis for support. 'She often confers with me before she passes a ruling. I am her test of the laws and customs. We all feel that people should be treated fairly and consistently. We cannot keep changing the rules and laws every time there is a problem. The people depend on us for consistency in the application of the law and the consequences for breaking the rule of law. They need to comprehend that there will be consequences for any misdeeds, before they commit them. In this way, it acts as a deterrent to wrongful behaviour.'

Zeus said nothing.

'Do you have any questions father?' Dike asked him.

'Yes, how do you keep track of the laws and customs to ensure that you remain consistent in their application?' he asked her.

'I have books in which we record the laws and judgments that have been determined,' she explained. 'We refer to them, and add to it as new laws are developed to suit each verdict, and we record the facts that led us to the outcome and the specified punishment. These are still in the formative stage, but we plan to have physical copies made of all these laws and the penalties they attract for breaking them, so that they can be taught and understood by everyone. Our humans used to be ignorant of the law. But through our efforts they all have a deep respect for them and appreciate the benefits to the society as a whole.'

'Tell your father about the speech you gave at the last town meeting,' Themis invited.

Dike cleared her throat and then drank some water. She drew in a deep breath and started, 'It sort of went something like this... "Listen to what you know in your mind is the right thing to do, and do not foster violence; for violence is bad for every man. Even the prosperous cannot easily bear its burden, as they are weighed down under it when they have fallen into delusion that they are above the law. The better path is to go on the side of justice; for justice beats outrage when it comes to the end of the race,'" she explained but then paused. 'There was more to it, but I think you get the gist of it,' she concluded.

'Thank you, Dike. I am sorry I missed your speech. Was it well received?'

'I think so,' she told him.

'I think it may have gone beyond the understanding of some of them,' conceded Themis. 'But many applauded, and there were many positive discussions among the humans afterward. We are still getting asked about it, so I gather it is an important topic of community discussion.'

'That is good. You have done well,' Zeus nodded his approval toward Dike as he smiled.

Zeus then looked at Nemesis. 'Nemesis, would you now share with us your part in development of human affairs?'

Nemesis rose from her chair. She hoped they were not all in trouble. She was suspicious of her father and that they were about to experience some impending doom. Trying to appear confident, she walked to the place where the others had given their presentations. 'I am Nemesis!' she explained.

'Thank you, Nemesis. We know who you are.'

Dike stifled a nervous laugh. She too felt the trepidation of Zeus's reveal. She looked at Themis and Astraea and they also seemed uneasy.

'I too seek to maintain the balance and good order among men. I differ slightly from Astraea and Dike as I seek out the injustice, often before it is apparent to the victims. Sometimes a man will prosper beyond reason. Those affected often do not realise that they have been robbed, cheated, or deceived. I seek out wrongdoers and bring them to justice. We then restore order and keep everything fair,' Nemesis explained.

Zeus nodded.

Nemesis continued. 'When there is an injury, the victim is alive and able to explain the cause of the incident. If there is a wrongdoing, then the perpetrator can be quickly brought to justice. However, when there is a death, the victim is speechless. If their death appears natural or as the result of an adventure that goes badly, the victim is mourned and honoured by their family. However, when the death occurs through a murder or a misdeed, then the guilty must be identified, prosecuted, and brought to justice and account for their crime.'

'I understand that you investigate the circumstances behind the crime or the death?'

'Yes.'

'So, you use your instincts to check things out when they do not seem right?'

'That is correct,' she answered.

'You must be exceptionally perceptive?' concluded Zeus.

'I would like to think that I am,' responded Nemesis.

'So, what do you conclude about today's events?' he asked her.

They all sat up sensing some enlightenment on why Zeus was so interested in them and their treatment of the humans.

'I... err,' Nemesis paused.

'Please feel free to speak your mind,' Zeus encouraged. 'You have not done anything wrong,' he added trying to reassure everyone. He smiled his most endearing smile and he was not dissuaded by the despondency that was clearly evident on their faces.

'One possibility is that you want to use Thera as a working example of how to deal with the issues of laws, crimes, and punishments, for the peoples of other places.'

'Good, please elaborate,' Zeus invited.

'Another is that the people of Thera have too many rights and liberties under law and you think it has gotten out of hand?'

'Excellent,' Zeus complimented her.

'Is that right?' Themis asked Zeus.

'The people of Thera are developing at a much faster rate than the people on the other islands and on the mainland,' he explained. 'I need to work out if this is in the best interests for the future of all the Gods and Goddesses. We do need humans to remain subservient to us. If we teach them how to create workable laws, and if we bestow upon them all their civil rights, they will grow in their independence, and I fear that will evolve to a point where they no longer need us,' he explained. 'They will become greedy and corrupt. It is in their nature. We may need to intercede and slow things down for the humans that live on Thera,' he added.

'We are considering writing a document, a charter, that defines and guarantees the rights and the protections under law to all of the citizens. It will state that they agreed to abide by the rules-based society as a condition of living on Thera. It will become a part of a formal ritual for newcomers to learn and agree to, before they can become accepted and integrated into our community.'

Zeus looked impassively about the room. He stared at his empty plate seemingly to contemplate something important. He then looked up, 'Let us have a break,' Zeus suggested. 'We should all freshen up before we will commence our tour of your island. I hope we will meet up the other visiting gods, and that I can observe your humans at work.'

The four women did not speak, but from the sadness on their faces they were clearly disheartened. It seemed that Zeus had plans to undo all their efforts to create a law-based society.

***

After they freshened up, they assembled at the front door of the palace. Themis's pregnant belly was already beginning to show and the three younger women were curious to learn what was happening to her.

'That is surprising. You appear to be about four months pregnant, mother,' noted Dike.

'I know, but I should not be. It only took last night.' Themis examined her pregnant belly. 'I am genuinely surprised that I am already this far along,' she replied and seemed perplexed.

'For this child, I have intentionally used super seed,' explained Zeus. 'Our son will have a unique place in our family, and he has a special purpose for the people of Thera.'

'What is it?' asked Themis.

'I will explain everything to you soon, Themis,' he countered. 'Just understand that this boy is a special god, and he has the ability to save the gods and protect our future.'

Zeus also had a reputation for being mysterious. The women examined each other's faces, trying to make sense of what their king was saying. They had nothing.

Astraea broke the awkward silence and asked Zeus. 'What would you like to see first father?'

'Let us wander about and see what is happening today in Akrotiri,' he suggested.

The four women and the king of the gods set off down the main street to "meet the people."

They walked down the gentle slope, past the trees and shrubs that lined the pathway that linked Themis's palace to the community. Themis had selected a location for her home so that the spread of humanity would never easily encroach on their privacy. A lightly wooded forest separated the goddesses from the townspeople's homes.

Their banter was casual and Zeus seemed to be cheerful and communicative. 'The air is crisp and fresh. This place reminds me of this little restaurant that Poseidon and I often frequent when we want to meet with each other.'

'We are fortunate that our citizens practice sanitation and hygiene, and that they lead a health focused lifestyle,' Themis explained. 'You will not detect human excrement or see any litter on our island.'

'Yes,' Zeus agreed. Everything is spotlessly clean and well ordered. You are all to be commended.'

Astraea added to the conversation. 'The elders and leaders have taken the on the responsibility of educating the others on the benefits of cleanliness, that it has become second nature for all Theran's.'

Zeus nodded.

Soon they came to a pen that held a large bull. There were teenagers standing and sitting near the pen. One young man encouraged by his friends climbed into the pen and called to the bull. Zeus stopped to watch as he always had a soft place in his heart for bulls and considered them to be kindred spirits, and had on occasion, morphed into its form.

The bull noticed the motioning and taunts of the young man and he quickly became agitated. The bull snorted and stomped his hooves in frustration at the nearness of the human's presence. Then the bull suddenly charged him. Standing face on to the charging bull, the young man dived onto the horns of the bull.

Nemesis shrieked, but the others stood watching in fascinated silence.

The man had grasped the two horns of the bull with his hands as he jumped up. He performed an acrobatic somersault over the bull's head, and twisted to land comfortably on the bulls back. The bull neared the fence and halted its charge. The man confidently slid off the beast's back and ran quickly to the wall of the pen where leapt up and over the side, before the bull could work out what had happened to him.

The other teenagers applauded and congratulated the young man's daring feat.

Zeus approached the young man.

'How often do you perform this stunt?' he asked.

'We choose not to overdo it my Lord,' he replied. 'It would tire out the bull if we did it too often. I actually like the beast and I do not want him to be harmed or to become too stressed. Besides, if the bull gets used to the stunt, he will get bored and will probably no longer charge at me,' he explained.

'Do you all perform this trick?' Zeus asked indicating the group of assembled teenagers.

'Yes,' he answered. 'With various bulls.'

'Why?'

'It is a symbol of our courage and skill as an acrobat,' he answered. 'We perform during festivals and special events. The six of us are a performance troupe. We act, sing, dance, juggle, and do somersaults as part of our show. The flip over the bull's head is part of the finale,' he explained to Zeus.

'I have never seen that done before,' Zeus commented.

'We have been doing this for quite some time,' explained the man.

Zeus looked at Themis and then at the man. 'I hope you never get hurt by the horns.'

'Yes, it is dangerous. We have lost one of our performers to the horns,' the man replied.

'Whilst I think you are brave and skillful to do so, I believe it be disrespectful to the bull.' He paused. 'Bulls and cattle are spiritually connected to our lands and people. The bull is my spirit beast.'

'Then we will remove them from our act, my Lord,' the young man offered and bowed in capitulation.

'That would be good,' replied Zeus. He smiled gratefully at the young man, seeming relieved that the unnecessary tormenting of the bulls would cease.

After a pause and a reassuring look at the bull to check if it was okay, Zeus turned and left the pen and continued his tour of the outer reaches of the township.

They came to a field that was full of wheat that appeared ready to harvest. Many men were working in the field. A mature lady was cutting the wheat and gathering into baskets. She was wearing her working clothes and supported a straw hat that was held in place by a scarf that was tied below her chin. As the group of gods came closer to her, she stopped her work, stood up straight, stretched, and stared at Zeus.

'Hello little brother,' she said.

'Demeter?' Zeus was surprised to see his sister. He left the others standing on the path and he walked down to greet his sister.

'Why are you on this island?' she sounded suspicious.

There was no hug or kisses exchanged between these two siblings. They had nothing in common, and she rarely approved of any of his plans, and she rarely had anything positive to say about his behaviour.

'It is good to see you also.'

'Do not be sarcastic with me. We are busy with much work to do,' she explained and then paused to stretch her back once more. 'I see you have a retinue of our young goddesses with you?' she indicated Themis and the others who had politely kept their distance.

'How well do you know them?'

'I know them quite well. Why do you ask?' She looked up and studied the women. 'Only two of them are pregnant. Are you slipping?'

Zeus did not take the bait.

'My son seems to be determined about a relationship with that one,' Demeter announced as she was indicating Astraea. 'For his sake, please leave that one untouched.'

Zeus smiled. It was a reasonable request, although it was unnecessary in Astraea's case.

'Why do you smile?' Demeter knew that there could be unanticipated consequences when he performed one of his mischievous grins.

Zeus exhaled a gust of air. 'You see, Astraea is a devotee to celibacy. She wants to remain a virgin all of her life. Advise Ploutos to find a willing and receptive woman to pursue.'

Demeter snorted. 'I know him well enough to remain unobtrusive in his trials of romance. The lessons he learns about unreciprocated love will come from her, not from me.'

Zeus nodded his support for her non-interference. He glanced about the fields. 'Are you responsible for all the wheat that flourishes on the island?' Zeus asked her.

'I am responsible for wheat everywhere,' she told him. 'We are experimenting on this island with a new type of wheat. We first start by improving the soil by planting lupins which we plough into the ground before we plant the wheat...' She paused. 'You are not really interested in agriculture, are you?' she inquired studying the bored expression on his face. 'Why do you bother to ask?'

'I do enjoy eating fresh bread,' he explained trying to look supportive and encouraging. 'Bread is made from wheat...'

'Please do not use your lame humour with me. I have heard enough of your wit to last me a lifetime. And in my case, that is a considerably long time,' she emphasised. 'What is the truth for your reason for being here?'

'I am interested in the development of the people and their skills on this island. They are far advanced compared to people of other settlements and towns on the mainland and the other islands.'

'What is that to you?'

'I am concerned,' he replied trying to keep vague. His sister had a habit of interrogating him for information that he found difficult to resist. He turned away from her and looked out at the ocean.

Demeter reached up and gently turned her brother to face her. 'These are essentially good people, Zeus,' she explained and then paused. 'Please do not interfere in this culture. Everything is working well for the people living here.' Demeter stretched once more. 'You would think that by being a goddess it would prevent me from having an aching back.'

Zeus said nothing. He reached out and turned his sister around. He folded her arms across her chest and then bodily lifted her up off the ground. They heard the creaking of bones readjusting and he then put her gently down. The relief for Demeter was instant.

'So, what are you doing here?' his sister persisted.

'I am investigating,' he replied.

'Why here? You should be at home on Mount Olympus with Hera and your family,' she suggested. 'Or you should be helping the people on the mainland. Those people deserve our help, Zeus. There is much fighting, and there are too many wars and much corruption. Inequity seems to be the only thing that is flourishing.

'The day-to-day issues that the humans have to deal with are not my concern. I will allow some humanitarian activities from the gods towards the humans. Just to help them toward some prosperity, but mostly to ensure their continued subservience to us. Being a patron for them, or bequeathing some benefit toward them, or being a sponsor of something crucial to them, endears the humans to us, and of that, I am supportive.'

'You fear their independence.'

'I do,' he responded. 'That is why I am here. You will not dissuade me from my mission,' Zeus warned her.

'Have you heard from Hestia?' she asked changing the subject.

'Nobody hears much from her,' Zeus replied. Hestia was their other sister.

'What about Poseidon and Hades?' she asked.

'What about them?' Zeus responded dryly.

'Do you meet up with them?'

'I see Poseidon often enough. Hades, never.'

'We are not much of a family, are we?' she mused.

'I prefer it that way,' stated Zeus. 'Anyway, I have things to do.' He motioned the four women to join him.

'Goodbye, Demeter,' Zeus said as he and the other four walked away.

They left the farmers tending the wheat and walked in silence for twenty or so minutes when they came to a field where men were running between two poles lodged in the ground. When they passed the second pole they slowed to a stop. A group of watchers applauded the man who ran first passed the pole.

Zeus watched in curious fascination. 'They appear to be running for no purpose,' he stated to no one specifically.

'Father, they are running to see who is the fastest,' Dike explained.

'Why?'

'For the honour,' She explained.

'I can see no battle?' Zeus was confused. 'Are they training to run into battle?'

'They compete without battle.'

'Without battle!' Zeus roared smiling.

'Yes father.'

Themis added. 'They also have events such as wrestling, boxing, jumping, spear throwing, throwing a shield...'

'Why?'

'For the honour, father,' Dike explained once more.

'They are skills needed for battle,' offered Nemesis.

'So, they are training for battle?' Zeus asked.

'No!' exclaimed Astraea. 'Fighting and battles is the last thing we want here.'

'What do they call these people who compete for no purpose?' asked Zeus mockingly.

'Competitors,' answered Themis.

'I believe they are called athletes, mother,' added Astraea.

'Oh, sorry,' Themis said.

'Athlete means "Prize seeker," doesn't it?' asked Zeus.

'Yes, I think so,' responded Astraea.

'It does,' confirmed Nemesis.

'What prizes do they get for winning?' asked Zeus patiently.

'A wreath made from Laurel leaves,' answered Astraea.

'And sometimes coin, food, and valuable gifts,' added Nemesis.

'We have a purpose-built gymnasium for athletes to use for training, father,' Dike explained.

'They exercise naked?' Zeus was intrigued. 'Are there female athletes?'

'Not yet father. There is some male resistance to females competing. I believe many male egos would be at risk of a male being bested by female.'

'Have the female athletes only compete against other females. Males should only compete against other males. Keep them separated,' Zeus suggested.

Themis came up close to Zeus and held him by the arm. 'You just want to see some naked women exercising.'

'I think that could become extremely popular,' Zeus enthused.

A man interrupted them as he came to speak with Themis. He was short and somewhat elderly. He appeared flustered, his face reddened from exertion.

'I beg forgiveness for intruding, O Themis,' he said looking at the ground.

'What do you want, Hesiod?' Themis replied.

'A brief audience if your eminence permits,' he asked meekly, looking at Zeus.

'Speak,' Zeus invited.

'Some of the prizes being offered to the athletes are getting to be a concern to the organisers,' he reported.

'How so?' asked Themis.

'One athlete has been promised several females for his personal use for his sexual pleasure,' he explained to them. 'Another has been promised the hand in marriage of the patron's daughter. But she does not love him or want him for her husband. The winner of this next race will receive more gold than I earn in a year,' he explained quickly with a hint of trepidation in his voice.

'I can see why they do not wage war,' observed Zeus. 'The spoils are far greater by just competing,' he paused. 'Tell me, why do they offer such extravagant rewards. What do the patrons gain?'

'The honour goes to the head of the village that represented as sponsors of the victor. Much glory goes to them and they all celebrate the win,' he explained.

'Vanity,' concluded Zeus.

'It is worse than that my lord,' Hesiod continued. 'Many athletes are forced to compete against their natural desire, and they are being punished if they do not, or if they fail to bring home glory to their patrons, they are often punished or even alienated.'

'Punished! How?' he demanded to know.

'Several of the men have been dismissed from service. One man was beaten and one man was executed!' he explained. 'His patron was so angry that he wanted to eliminate that man from breeding and producing incapable sons.'

'Really?' said Zeus.

'What else, Hesiod? asked Themis.

'There is much gambling on the outcome, and often the races are predetermined,' he continued.

'Nemesis!' roared Zeus.

Nemesis stepped forward. 'Yes, father.'

'I want you to start an investigation on these "games." ordered Zeus. 'They do not seem to be much fun for the competitors, or fair on the audience.'

'At once,' Nemesis accepted.

Hesiod bowed to offer his gratitude, and he then discretely moved away from Zeus and the Goddesses.

Zeus motioned to Themis to come closer, and she immediately moved toward him. In soft tones he admonished Themis. 'It would appear that you and the others were unaware of these misdeeds.'

'Yes, I knew nothing, and the others would have told me if they had any inkling that this was happening,' she agreed.

'I believe that you have much less control over your humans than you imagined.

Themis turned pale. She was beginning to fear that Zeus was right.

***

The group set off toward the centre of Akrotiri, when they heard a male voice calling.

'Astraea! Astraea!' the voice yelled as the man ran down the dusty path toward them.

They turned to see that it was Ploutos coming toward them.

Puffing, he slowed his pace as he came nearer to them. 'Uncle,' he nodded his greeting to Zeus.

'Ploutos,' Zeus acknowledged. He accepted that he barely knew the man.

'Hello Themis, Dike, Nemesis,' he said to the others.

Dike and Nemesis were both smiling at Ploutos as he managed to manoeuvre himself to be closer to Astraea. She was clearly uncomfortable with his proximity and recoiled at his panting. The two other young women were enjoying seeing Astraea struggle being so near to a man that was so obviously infatuated with her.

Themis looked at him with a degree of annoyance. 'Ploutos,' she responded. 'We are busy showing Zeus about the island. What do you want?' she asked him impatiently.

'Just to speak with Astraea, if I may?' he asked expectantly.

'She is beside you. Speak to her,' Themis invited.

'Er... privately if I may?' he added.

Zeus huffed and walked away. Themis and the others slowly turned and followed him. They looked at Astraea for any signs of discomfort, but she motioned them away. 'I will catch up with you in a moment,' she assured them.

'My darling ... Astraea. All I want is to spend some time with you,' declared Ploutos. 'I thought, well, if you got to know me better...' he let the words hang and seemed sadly pathetic.

'Zeus has recently adopted me,' Astraea informed him. 'Whilst he is here, it is a daughter's duty to attend to her father.'

'But you have been avoiding me ever since I arrived on the island,' he blurted.

'I am not attracted to you, Ploutos,' she explained.

'Is there someone else?'

'No. What makes you ask that?'

'Well, if not me, then who?'

'Who? What are you on about?'

'Do you have a boyfriend, a mate, a man in your life that you might feel is suitable as a potential husband?'

'Why would I want one of those?'

'Oh,' Ploutos tried vainly to remain buoyant. 'A companion, a friend, a lover...'

'Ooh, yuck,' she winced.

'Everyone wants to be loved,' he stood there with his arms wide inviting embrace, but she stepped back from him and he was suddenly feeling silly, and so he let his arms drop.

'Listen carefully to me, Ploutos. Do not think about me. I am not interested and I never will be. Go away and go find a pretty nymph and have some fun. You deserve to find love with someone that can reciprocate.'

'But you said you liked me?'

She studied him remembering. Yes, I did, but it was a friendly expression, not an invitation to pursue a romance with me. Please understand that I am sure that you are a charming man, but I am not interested in having any type of relationship with you.'

'Do you prefer girls?' he accused her.

'I would not know. I have not considered that as an option for me,' she paused glaring at him, and then continued. 'Now go away. I really must catch up with the others…'

'I am rich,' he boasted. 'Many women….'

'Do you think that I would fall in love with you just because you have wealth?' she asked accusingly.

'Err…' he was clearly uncertain off how to respond.

'Besides, I am a goddess and therefore wealth is irrelevant to me, and it should be to you also,' she accused.

'It is exhilarating to know that my fortune grows through my endeavours. Is it wrong to share that knowledge and experience with others?'

'It is your love of wealth and greed that you are teaching to humans that is causing the numerous problems, that we are now forced to deal with. Our humans were content, happy, generous, and loving, until you introduced them to coins!' she admonished him sternly. 'Now too many of them love wealth more than they care about family or friends.'

'They can have both. Much profit comes from equitable collaboration. I truly believe that they all should profit from their enterprises,' he defended.

'And I do not. So there, you now have a good reason to leave me alone!' she turned and ran off to catch up with the others.

Ploutos stood alone and despondent. He examined the ground feeling much like a tragic victim of unrequited love, and he was disappointed that it had not gone as he had hoped. But, Ploutos was also resilient, and so he decided that he would rise up and welcome her challenge. In time she would respect him, his mission, and his values. One day she would want him as much as he wanted her. He would remain positive, and persistent, and forever vigilant for the perfect opportunity to win her devotion and unconditional love.

***

Astraea soon caught them up as they were walking slowly. They had stopped to take in the many vistas the high points on the island offered.

'It is a lovely Island,' Zeus commented as he, Themis, and the three younger women set off once more.

They walked in silence for a while.

'Where are we going now?' Zeus asked Themis.

'We are going to sit in on a meeting of the civic leaders,' she told him. 'They meet weekly to discuss significant events, pass by-laws and make resolutions.'

He stared at her so she continued. 'The councillors are chosen by the people, and they have the confidence to make fair decisions about aspects that affect everyone.'

'Do you participate in these meetings?' Zeus wanted to know.

'Only when I am invited,' she answered smiling.

'What causes them to want to invite you?' Zeus asked.

'Generally, when there is a stalemate in their reasoning that requires independent assessment and direction, they come to me,' she answered. 'If they get locked in argument and cannot agree, they ask me to hear both sides of the situation. I weigh up their points and offer my thoughts. That often resolves the problem, but not always,' she explained.

'What happens then?'

'If the issue requires more investigation and deliberation, then the decision is deferred. If the outcome is important and it affects the majority of people, then the citizens of the island get a vote,'

'Men and women?'

'Certainly,' she replied and smiled at the puzzled expression on his face. 'On Thera, both male and female adult citizens get a vote, after all they are involved and equally affected by decisions and outcomes.'

'Slaves, foreigners, convicted people, and the poor are not allowed to partake in voting,' added Dike as she stepped ahead and opened the great door to the meeting chamber. The others filed in passed her and she followed them in.

The human statesmen stopped talking when they saw Zeus, Themis, and the three other goddesses enter the room. They stood and bowed in respect.

'Please continue,' offered Zeus. 'Don't mind us.'

One man stepped forward. 'Forgive me lord for questioning your presence, but is there something that we may assist you with?' he asked.

Zeus looked at them benevolently, or at least he thought he did. 'What is your current topic of conversation?' he asked.

The people were silent.

They offered Zeus a chair and some other chairs were brought in to accommodate all five visitors in some comfort. They sat and a tray with cups of wine were offered to each of them. Only Zeus reached forward and accepted a drink from them. He motioned a salute with his cup and took a sip. He liked it, and so he drank some more. He indicated his approval of the quality of the wine and the host smiled knowingly.

Finally, a woman spoke in a clear and confident voice. 'My Lord, my name is Helena. I am wife to Thabo. They are talking about excluding women from voting in matters affecting the people of Thera.'

'Please continue,' invited Zeus.

'After many years of equal rights and equal representation, with women proving that females can contribute to the decision making in affairs that affect all of us,' she paused for breath. 'They now propose that we voluntarily exclude ourselves to only household management. They (pointing at the men) do not want us to engage in matters of business, commerce, civil matters, laws, or education!'

The others remained quiet.

'Are the women on Thera educated?' asked Zeus.

'We are!' several of them declared.

'At a great cost, my Lord,' interjected a male elder.

'Please, present your rational,' invited Zeus.

'When a woman involves herself in civic affairs, her duties in the home become less of a priority to her, and as a result, they are often neglected. You see, the family unit suffers. Also, as we know that some women fall under the influence of men other than their husbands. Helena has been seen spending much time with Sacless!'

'It is true that we have spent time together. We have much business to discuss. My husband is an exporter and deals with the sea merchants and Sacless is the man that controls the harbour.'

'And while your husband is trading, Sacless is the man docking in your port!' exclaimed a man loudly.

'That's a lie,' Helena screamed.

Another man stepped forward. 'My lord,' he started. 'My name is Vaster. I have been on this council for many years. Both men and women have enjoyed an equal say, and have had equal representation on this council for all that time,' he paused. 'Most recently, the women of Thera seem to us to be losing their desire to concentrate on family needs, values, and family unity.'

Vaster glanced about the room for moral support. The other men were nodding their agreement. Helena was still fuming.

Vaster continued, 'There has also been an increase in moral disease. Extra marital sexual activities as a result of female freedoms, has resulted in widespread sharing of genital afflictions. It is also becoming a major problem.'

The other men continued to nod in complete support.

Zeus waited until there was calm before he addressed the council members. 'In all other lands, women do not participate in the affairs of men,' he told them. He looked about the room. They remained silent, listening intently so he continued. 'Women have always been kept busy with domestic activities. They care for the husband, the home and their children. They are responsible for a great many things, and they should always be respected and revered by society for their role in nurturing and developing their children into responsible adults. Often husbands must toil away from home to provide for their family. They make great sacrifices to be a good provider. They deserve a home to rest, feed, fornicate, and feel safe inside at all times without worry of a betrayal by their chosen partner.'

The women councillors appeared contrite. They could sense where this was heading and they now felt that their freedom of assembly, the right to vote, and their participation in civil affairs might be coming to an end.

Zeus paced the room and then continued. 'However,' he paused and the women looked up and men appeared worried. 'This is your island. Themis and the others,' he indicated Astraea, Dike and Nemesis, 'are here to guide and assist you. It is your vote that determines the rights of citizens.'

There was more silence.

Zeus continued. 'You could return to the old ways. Men are much better at dealing with outside issues as they spend more time attending to them. Women are better home makers because they spend more time in the home,' he paused to let his opinion soak in. 'Whilst it is ultimately up to the people of Thera, and I accept that the decision is yours alone to make, I however, believe that you should return to the tried and tested ways of masculine governance that are practiced by all other Greek peoples.'

As Zeus sat down, the hum of murmured discussion began in earnest.

One man stood up to speak his opinion. 'The problem with many women voters, is that they are not all that interested in the outcome, so for many of them, they vote as their husbands instruct them to. By excluding women, and low born males from the vote, we will actually be improving the value of the outcome, as only enlightened people will be affecting the decision, and therefore informed electors will vote in such a way to optimise the benefits to all.' He checked the room before he continued. 'Everyone should be allowed to vote for who they choose to represent their interests on this council. It is up to those seeking election to educate their electors into the benefits of giving them their support. We do not need community voting on all aspects of our activities, but we do need voting in the selection of which persons hold office that have a mandate on how we are governed.'

There was a murmur of agreement.

'My Lord,' Vaster spoke above the noise and everyone respectfully quietened to listen. 'Fellow councillors,' Vaster had both hands raised to indicate to all that he had the floor. 'I propose that we do have a vote,' he suggested. 'We should vote on a motion that a general referendum should be held to determine whether women should continue to get equal representation on civil matters.'

'Hear, hear!' was the cry.

Vaster declared. 'A white bean is a vote for the referendum to remove women from the process. A black bean signifies that we remain a gender equal community with voting to be held to determine representation.'

They queued for the bowls containing coloured beans. Each councillor drew a black bean and a white bean. They then passed an amphora that had a secure slotted lid. Each person deposited one of their two beans into the amphora.

When each of the councillors had voted, the amphora was opened by two people. The beans were divided by colour and clearly the black beans outnumbered the white.

'The vote is determined.' stated Vaster. 'We will remain a gender equal society.'

Zeus stood up. 'Thank you for allowing me the privilege of witnessing the good governance of the people of Thera. Your processes are well ahead of the thinking in other political regions.'

The group applauded Zeus's comments.

'I am sorry, but we must leave you.' He motioned the others to join him. 'Themis and her team...' he smiled at the others, 'are giving me the guided tour of your lovely island.'

The group applauded once more.

Vaster held up is hands for silence.

'My lord, thank you for your kind words and wise contribution,' he paused. 'It is comforting to know that you believe that the Theran's are an enlightened people, and that we are well ahead of other communities in recognising women's contribution to society, as equals.'

Zeus said nothing. His smile was his response.

Vaster continued. 'The men and women who rule Thera have brought about intellectual thinking that is obviously way ahead of the rest of the world. We have introduced public art, community theatre, public poetry, and song and dance. We freely debate issues and they are decided by popular majority. We continue to develop our constitutional rights, the obligations of the citizens, and a set of laws which govern the behaviour of all our people.'

As the king of the gods and the four goddesses left the building, they overheard someone continue the self-adulation. 'We possess the vision, empathy, integrity, and have the ability to motivate and inspire our people.'

'Hear, hear,' was the chorused response.

As they walked away, Themis turned and asked Zeus, 'What was your impression of their process of government?'

'They did not understand what I was telling them...' he replied but left the rest of his words unspoken.

Astraea added 'They want to establish their own courts with their own judges! They want grievances heard and the plaintive bound by the verdict.'

'We will be out of a job,' Themis added laughing.

'They have not yet addressed the issue of communicable diseases,' Zeus said indignantly. 'They will not be interested in good government when their genitals fall off,' he added dryly.

'There is one man who is working on a solution to that problem,' Themis advised him.

Zeus examined her.

'We are taking you to meet him,' she added.

As the group walked through the streets of Akrotiri, its citizens who were now aware of Zeus presence in their community, filed out of their homes to wave and greet him. Zeus seemed to stand taller when he was being admired by mortals, and he acknowledged the praises and well wishes of the people who cheered him.

Themis's belly continued to grow and she now appeared to be close to full term. She held back as Zeus strode forward through the crowds of happy people.

Nemesis and Dike assisted her.

'Astraea,' said Themis.

'Yes mother,' she replied.

'Please take your father to meet Gorontalo,' she asked of her. 'I will have to return to the palace chambers as my belly is slowing me down and wearing me out.'

Astraea rushed forward and caught up with Zeus.

'Father.'

He turned to look at her.

'Mother is exhausted,' she explained. 'Her pregnancy is now well advanced and she needs to rest.'

Zeus stopped. He turned and watched Themis staggering awkwardly. She was being assisted by both Dike and Nemesis.

He walked up to them. 'My dear, I am so sorry,' he apologised. 'I should have notice how much your pregnancy has advanced.'

'I think I am about to drop this cargo!' Themis declared. 'My contractions have started.'

'We should return to your chambers!' Zeus agreed.

'No, you and Astraea continue with your tour. Dike and Nemesis will assist me to get home and they will care for me.'

'But...'

'You have been useless for all my other births. You will not be any different with this one.'

'Well...'

'Go on.'

'As you wish,' and he performed a polite bow in acquiescence.

Themis, ably assisted by Dike and Nemesis, headed toward the palace. Zeus and Astraea watched them until they rounded a corner.

'You were married to Themis once, weren't you?' Astraea asked her adopted father.

'Yes, briefly,' he agreed. 'I think my ex-wives decide among themselves as to who will step up to be my current wife. I never let them get in the way of what I am doing, so I do not concern myself with it too much,' he admitted.

'But... Hera is your wife?' she asked him quizzically.

'That is right, but do not ask me why, as I cannot fathom it,' he paused, 'We are often at odds and she is quick to tell me when she does not approve of what I say, or with what I plan to do.'

'So...?' Astraea let the question hang.

'So, I do not tell her,' Zeus explained as he smiled.

***

Childbirth was not a new experience for Themis. She had had quite a few babies with Zeus and several others as well. The gestation period was normally nine months like mortal woman. The Goddesses could choose how long it took to make a baby and three months seemed fine to Themis. But the fact that this one was ripe to pop sooner than twenty-four hours after conception did not surprise her too much. With Zeus as the father, anything could happen and often did. She concluded that this child, hastily implanted into her by Zeus, had a special purpose.

'How you doing, mother?' asked Dike. They were nearing the palace. Nemesis had rushed on ahead to get help.

'I am okay,' she smiled but she was in obvious discomfort.

'We are nearly there,' reassured Dike.

They entered the room and some palace servants rushed to assist the women. A litter appeared and Themis rested down onto it. She was carried into her bed chamber.

'The contractions have increased,' she informed them.

'Shall we fetch Eileithyia?' asked Nemesis.

'No need,' she replied. I think there will be few problems delivering this one.'

Themis transferred herself to her bed. Nemesis and Dike dismissed the staff and helped Themis get comfortable. Themis moved her legs up and apart. She cursed Zeus and the two others laughed.

Themis then laughed also, and then stopped abruptly.

'It is coming!' she told them.

Eileithyia, daughter of Zeus and Hera and goddess of childbirth entered the room. It was as if she materialized from thin air.

'I heard your call,' she explained. She approached the bed and looked calmly at Themis.

'I did not know you were pregnant, Themis,' said Eileithyia casually.

'It only happened yesterday,' Themis explained.

'Father?'

'Yes, he... augh!' she cut short of her explanation as a massive contraction racked Themis's body.

Nemesis and Dike watched in fascination. They stared at the baby's head that was now appearing from the birth canal between Themis's legs. This was a new experience for both of them.

'Oh good,' announced Eileithyia. 'The baby is in the cephalic presentation.'

Nemesis and Dike looked at each other uncomprehendingly, and they shrugged as they were reassured by Eileithyia nodding that it was okay.

'Gently but firmly push down,' Eileithyia instructed.

'I know what I am doing,' Themis managed to keep a civil tone.

'I believe you,' Eileithyia replied remaining calm.

The baby continued to emerge as Themis maintained a steady heave and she pushed her baby out into the world. The head was now out and the baby lifted is chin away from its chest and the baby's body started to rotate. Then the shoulder appeared and the baby slid away from its mother and onto the sheet.

'It is a boy,' announced Nemesis.

'Would you cut the cord please Dike?' Themis asked her daughter calmly.

Dike cut the cord as Eileithyia pressed a clamp on the cord near to the baby's abdomen. She quickly washed the birth fluids away from the baby's face. The baby was alert and looked about the room. There was no screams or fuss normally associated with a human childbirth. Themis experienced some discomfort throughout the process. The speed of the pregnancy had not allowed her body to adjust properly to the birthing demands that were placed on her body.

'Is this typical of a birthing experience?' Dike asked Eileithyia.

'Yes,' she smiled. 'Well, it is for Goddesses,' she added.

'I have heard that mortals scream for hours during childbirth?'

'For human women it can be a lengthy and extremely painful experience,' she explained. 'Goddesses from Mount Olympus can choose not to be burdened with mortal pains and aches.'

'So, I can have a delivery like mum?' asked Nemesis. She looked concerned.

'Of course you can,' she smiled.

Themis laughed at Nemesis. 'My poor darling. Did you think you think that you would experience mortal childbirth?'

'I did not know what to think,' admitted Nemesis.

'This is her first pregnancy,' added Dike.

'Could you arrange some warm water and towels please?' Eileithyia asked to either of them. 'I would like to clean this young man.' She examined the baby and smiled, as she passed the baby to Themis who held him to her chest.

Nemesis left the room and came back moments later with two female staff members. They carried basins, warm water in jugs, and towels. Eileithyia took the baby and carefully washed him as Themis attended to her own clean-up assisted by Dike. They also changed the sheets and resorted the bedding.

'Congratulations,' offered Eileithyia. She passed the baby back to his mother. Eileithyia examined the afterbirth and was satisfied that all was well. She nodded to Themis indicating that it was so.

'Thank you, Eileithyia,' Themis said sounding grateful.

'It was a pleasure,' Eileithyia smiled and she seemed genuinely pleased to be of assistance. She then bowed, and faded from the room.

'How weird that must have felt for her,' Dike commented.

'How do you mean?' Nemesis questioned.

'Helping to deliver your own brother to a woman that is not your mother. She is normally furious with her father's infidelities.'

Nemesis had not thought of that. Her eyes widened in the realisation that it was so.

Presently the three women were relaxing. Themis had the baby boy to her breast.

'Normally... I do not produce breast milk this quickly,' she explained, sounding a bit surprised. 'It is just as well that I can, as he has quite the appetite!' she exclaimed.

'I think he has grown,' observed Dike.

'Yes, he has,' agreed Themis. She seemed puzzled.

'Do you have a name for him?' asked Nemesis.

'I thought I would wait for Zeus to see him. He explained that there were special plans for this boy.'

'It is intriguing,' agreed Nemesis.

'The baby suckled contently and for a while they all enjoying just watching him.

'Well, I think I am empty on this one my darling,' she told the baby and swapped him to the other breast. The baby barely noticed. He latched on to the other nipple and continued feeding happily. Later Themis rested him from feeding and sat him up for a burp, which when it came, it was so loud that they all laughed in surprise.

***

While Themis was busy giving birth to her son, Zeus and Astraea came across a group of people preparing for a wedding ceremony. From a discreet distance, Astraea explained the local custom to her father. 'Weddings on Thera are steeped in ritual. A bride, who is often as young as thirteen years of age, is considered ready for marriage as soon as her menstrual cycle begins. The first part of the ritual is when the bride formally offers all of her toys, and dolls, and other childish things to Artemis as a symbol of her maturity. She then offers a fig-urine of a woman baking bread...'

'Hesitia,' Zeus added interrupting.

'That is right, she is your sister,' Astraea added unnecessarily. 'This marks the significant shift in her life, and the start of her new role as a housewife,' she added.

Zeus was listening intently, but he said nothing else.

Astraea continued. 'Before she marries, she bathes in clean water, she is groomed and perfumed. Her family apply red ochre to her lips and chalk to lighten her complexion. She is dressed in an ankle length yellow linen dress that is fastened at the shoulder with a brooch. She wears a belt around her waist so that the dress gathers neatly around her body. On her feet she wears leather sandals. Her hair is straightened and it is held up with pins and a headband. She is also wears a pendant necklace with matching earrings, and silver bracelets.'

'It would seem that they go through a lot of trouble. None of my weddings were that complicated.'

'Were your brides looking their best for you at your weddings?' she asked mordantly.

'I guess so,' he replied as he examined her facial features that were evidently challenging him to concede to the beauty of every bride, and respect her for her wedding day preparations. 'I think I was more focused on the honeymoon ritual than the actual wedding ceremony.'

Her facial expression rapidly changed and she turned away, blushing. Zeus smiled and sensed a small victory.

She drew a deep breath and continued, 'The bridegroom is often much older than his bride. In this case he is thirty and he has proven himself to be wealthy enough to claim her as his bride. He has convinced her parents that he can provide for her. During a brief ceremony, the father will give his daughter to the groom. They will be carried to the groom's home and she will be welcomed by the groom's mother. His mother will carry a burning torch to light their way and when they arrive, she will ceremoniously welcome the newly married couple into her home. They will kneel together before the hearth, where they will be showered with chopped dried fruits, seeds, and grains as symbols of their future prosperity. Then there is feasting and drinking with close family. During the following days, friends will arrive with gifts that will help the couple start their married life together.'

'When do they...?'

'Consummate? On their first night together,' Astraea answered quickly as she had anticipated his question.

'Often, he will show the blood from their intercourse to his family, as proof of her maidenhood and of their congress. She must agree to receive him to complete the wedding contract. It is best for her to endure a small embarrassment and remove all doubt.'

'Why do they have all this elaborate preparation and fuss?' Zeus was incredulous.

'Bigamy is forbidden, adultery is rare, and divorce is uncommon. It is essential to all vested parties to get it right the first time.'

'Whatever makes them happy.'

They stayed to watch the ceremony from a discreet distance.

Astraea thought that the man was looking lovingly into his bride's eyes. He seemed exceptionally contented that she will soon be his wife. This girl was young and she hoped for her sake that her mother had prepared her for this next phase of her life.

Zeus thought that the man was looking a little too lustfully into the girl's eyes. He acted excitedly and looked delighted that he will soon be having his way with her. He hoped for the man's sake that he was skilled at the art of lovemaking, as sex between them will rapidly reduce in frequency if she is dissatisfied or hurt by his performance.

The family of the bride noticed the gods observing them. They waved in excitement and beckoned them to come and join them.

Zeus smiled and waved as he took Astraea's arm and led her in the other direction, quickly rounding a corner.

Astraea laughed at Zeus's reluctance of being invited to the human wedding ceremony.

Zeus snorted indignantly.

'You would have been made very welcomed at that family event,' Astraea admonished gently. 'Now you have offended them.'

'They do not know who I am,' Zeus retorted.

'Oh, they know who you are. The island is abuzz with talk of your visit. Everyone is speculating as to why you are here,' she explained and her eyebrows rose as she examined him enquiringly.

Zeus would not allow himself to be led into a response. He smiled and nodded knowingly.

They walked in silence for some time when they came to a public bench that overlooked a stunning vista of the rocky coastline and the clear blue ocean. It was a wonderfully sunny day that had just the right sea breeze to keep things from feeling too warm.

Zeus invited her to sit down, and they sat together in silence enjoying the view.

He eventually cleared his throat and turned toward her. 'Please do not take this the wrong way, but I have observed that the islanders do not pay you much respect or homage considering that you are a goddess.'

'How do you mean?' she asked now puzzled.

'You, your sisters, Themis, the other gods and goddess that work here, and those that visit the island from Mount Olympus are not revered. They do not treat you with awe and respect. There are no shrines or temples in your honour. They do not pray to you, or sing your godly praises. It is like you are treated kindly, and respectfully, but more like you are one of the family, and not a goddess with significant powers.'

She smiled at him. She decided to be patient with him and calmly explain to him the way things were done on the island. 'You see father. The general consensus among the goddesses and gods that live and work here is that we are here to guide and advise the mortals on how to live good productive and happy lives without using anything other than reasoning. On the mainland the humans live in fear of the gods. There, they will be punished for their errant behaviour and lack of worshipping of the gods and goddesses. Here, on our island, we teach self-sufficiency and the benefits of a fair and democratic way to expand a society as a place where everyone contributes their best because it is the right thing to do.'

'Do you believe your plan is working?' Zeus asked. His tone was gentle as if he was genuinely interested in the success of this approach.'

'Oh, father it is,' she smiled, appearing proud of their achievements.

'Have you experience any setbacks to your grand plan?'

'Some. You see, ignorance can be cured by learning as long as the benefits are acceptable, but arrogance is a lifelong sentence and cannot be cured. For those people, we channel their arrogance through the application of the greater moral good. In this way the majority defeat the minority, and so they capitulate as they have no choice but to do so,' she explained and paused to let her words soak in. She was proud of her islanders moral and ethical behaviour. 'Some people have left our island, vowing never to return. We say goodbye and hope that they do not.'

'Your plan might work in a small closed community like this one, but it will never work on the mainland,' Zeus said trying to share his opinion as kindly as he could.

'Father, we will never actually know if what you say is true until we try. Humanity might surprise you.'

Zeus studied her earnest expression, but he remained quiet.

***

After sitting in silence for some time, Astraea suddenly stood up. She reached for her father's hand and pulled him to his feet. They continued their inspection of the community.

On Therea, there were several main ways for a person to be gainfully employed within the community. People were either a merchant trader, a land owner farmer, a fisherman, or an engineer, craftsman, or a tradesman. A few armed soldiers were required to keep the peace and to attended to civil matters. There was no need for a military presence, as they had no enemies.

A skilled farmer's produce would feed more people than just his immediate family, so they were highly respected. Trades people made things and kept thinks working. They were taught their skills by their father or a mentor, and they traded their skills and services for coin or food. Trades included perfumers, weavers, tailors, cobblers, marble cutters, builders, carpenters, blacksmiths, tanners, and leather men.

The trades people occasionally purchased slaves from the sea merchants that visited the island. They helped to do the heavy dirty repetitive work, and they filled the gap in any labour shortage as their economy was thriving and trade was vibrant and profitable. They trained them as they supervised their work, and they often worked closely with them. Most slaves quickly earned their freedom, an eventually they became accepted and respected members of the community.

When they came to a potter's workshop, they stopped to watch the activity. The pottery was made by craftsmen who used a large stone wheel that was balanced on a turning shaft. They watched a potter as he sat on a stool at the wheel about thirty centimeters above the ground. The potter deposited a quantity of wet red clay onto the wheel and then used a foot pedal to start spinning the wheel up to a comfortable speed. He carefully shaped the clay into an urn. When it was close to becoming the required shape, he maintained slower movements of the wheel by using his other foot on a disk that was at ground level. This action allowed him to alternate the direction of the wheel while he performed the finishing touches. It was vigorous and dexterous work.

Another potter was making a finished urn glossy. He added ash to clay and water and painted the areas he wanted blackened. When fired in the kiln, the paint would make those areas black and the rest would remain red clay coloured. Red figure ware was where the potter painted the background in black and left the figures in natural clay. These were keenly sought after and they created much excitement among shoppers and collectors alike.

Zeus observed five figurines that were set above the workshop. They were each about the size of a ten-year-old, and they were protected from the elements with several layers of glaze.

'Do you know who they represent?' he asked Astraea pointing at the clay statues.

'No,' she replied. 'Would you like me to ask them?' she offered.

'No, no, it is all right,' he stopped her. 'I'll explain. They represent the five Daemones Ceramici.'

'The wha...?'

'Five malevolent spirits that plague all potters,' he laughed. 'These figurines are a tribute to them, and they are prominently displayed to ask them to leave this workshop alone.'

I never knew,' Astraea volunteered.

Zeus laughed again. He pointed to each in turn. 'That one is Syntribos, the shatterer, next to him is Smaragos, the smasher, then Asbetos the charrer, and Sabaktes the destroyer.' He paused pointing at the last figurine trying to remember.

'Omodamos!' contributed the potter that they had been watching. He rose off of his seat and walked up to Zeus and Astraea.

'Ah yes, Omodamos, that is right. He is the one apprentices use to account for their mistakes.'

Both Zeus and the potter roared in laughter at Zeus's joke.

Astraea looked puzzled.

'When an apprentice fires his work and it fails, he blames Omodamos for the "crudeness of the bake",' the potter explained. He bent down and lifted an example. The misshaped urn looked glum and sad and this clearly amused Zeus and the potter. 'You understand? According to the apprentice, it is never their fault.' he explained smiling.

'There may be a demand for this,' Astraea offered hopefully.

The potter re-entered his workshop and returned with an urn that was decorated with the image of Zeus holding up many lightning bolts and looking fierce. The target of his lightning was a group of whimpering monsters that Zeus was defeating. He passed it to Zeus who accepted it graciously.

Zeus held and examined urn in interest. 'It is… all… true,' he concluded with a smile.

Astraea and the potter laughed.

He offered the urn back to the potter, but the man immediately returned the urn to Zeus. 'A gift my lord,' he declared proudly.

Zeus received the urn with an appreciative and respectful bow. They waved and turned to continue their tour.

They soon came across a Blacksmiths workshop. Blacksmiths made all types of agricultural tools, cooking ware, and weapons. By combining metals, they could make them harder and sturdier. By adding tin to copper to form bronze they were able to make metal objects more durable. Iron was even stronger and becoming popular in sword making.

In one corner of the smith was a tribute to Zeus's son, Hephaestus, God of fire and metal working.

Zeus nodded at the tribute. 'My son is good man and he is a god to be respected. He does amazing work but...' he paused.

'But?' asked Astraea.

'Why he ever wanted to marry Aphrodite is still beyond me?'

Astraea did not comment. The male preoccupation for beautiful women did not impress her. She knew their marriage ended in disaster.

Zeus picked up a sword from a display rack. He was clearly impressed with the workmanship. He passed the urn to Astraea and stepped out into the opening. A crowd quickly gathered as Zeus worked the sword through a series of swordsmanship exercises. The blade often came close to an eager audience member, and they hurriedly stepped back with nervous laughter. Presently he stopped. He bowed and received a burst of applause. Zeus returned the sword to the display.

The blacksmith stood beaming. He picked out the sword an held it reverently up to Zeus. 'A gift for you, my lord.' he offered.

Zeus studied the man. He was tall and muscular. His blackened face and arms highlighted the white of his eyes. His left arm had many burns and scorch marks on it as did his apron.

'Thank you, but no,' Zeus replied. 'I have more swords than any one god can possibly need.'

The blacksmith appeared sullen.

Zeus drew in a deep breath and continued, 'And for some reason, when I meet a foe in battle, I always end up owning theirs!' he roared, addressing the crowd theatrically.

The crowd and the blacksmith burst out with laughter and they applauded Zeus's joke.

He waved at the crowd and made to leave.

'I think we should go and check on Themis,' suggested Astraea.

'And maybe we can lose this crowd,' Zeus added quietly.

Zeus retrieved the urn and he and Astraea bid goodbye to the people, and they turned and headed back to Themis's palace.

'You see father. The Theran's do love and respect us gods. You saw the images on the potters' work that clearly shows their respect for the divine from Mount Olympus.'

'That is purely for the export market my dear. Not for personal use. Trust me, they are nonbelievers.'

***

As they came up to the palace they were greeted by Nemesis.

'Hello, I was just coming to find both of you,' she told them.

'How is Themis?' Zeus asked.

'Great!' Nemesis reported. 'She and the baby are both fine.'

'Boy or girl?' asked Astraea.

'It is a boy,' she answered. 'Themis wanted to wait for you to return before giving him his name,' she added to Zeus.

'Lead the way Nemesis,' Zeus ordered. 'I await meeting our new champion with eager anticipation,' he said and was smiling.

Zeus and Astraea followed Nemesis up to the palace, walked through the vestibule, turned left and headed directly for Themis's bed chamber.

As they passed some servants, Zeus turned to them and bellowed. 'Prepare us some food and wine. Get some musicians organised, for tonight we feast and celebrate!'

Nemesis and Astraea looked at each other grinning. It was good to see Zeus happy.

Zeus spotted the exchange. 'I am hungry,' he declared by way of an explanation. As he passed a table ladened with the remnants of cleared food and wine, Zeus spotted a cup with some wine remaining. He gathered it up, examined it, sniffed it, and then consumed it.

They quietly entered into Themis chamber. Dike looked up them and rushed to Astraea and they hugged.

'Our baby brother is handsome,' she told her.

As they approached the mother and her newborn baby, Themis offered the boy to his father. Zeus was still holding the cup so he passed it to Nemesis who examined it to find it empty. He then gathered his son and cradled him with practiced confidence.

'Hello my son,' he looked him over. 'He is exceptionally handsome, just like his father,' he declared to the four women.

They laughed.

'He is a hefty lad,' Zeus observed.

'Oh, one feed on each breast and he seemed to triple in size. It would be easy to believe that he was a one-year-old.'

Zeus did not seem surprised or concerned with the boy's rapid growth. 'Themis, I want to name the boy, Lantis.'

'Lantis,' repeated Themis.

'Yes,' confirmed Zeus. 'Please understand that he has a special purpose for the people of Thera.'

The women did not speak.

'For a brief time, he will be known as the god of this island.' He paused. 'But the people must not be told of him just yet,' he added mysteriously.

'I do not understand,' said Themis.

Zeus turned to Dike, Astraea, and Nemesis. 'Girls, please give us a moment. I need to talk with Themis privately.'

They left the room and Zeus outlined his plan for Lantis, and the people of Thera to Themis.

***

Nemesis, Dike, and Astraea, walked together into the feasting area. Servants were completing the buffet style display with trays of fresh fruits, vegetables, hot and cold meats, sauces, cheese, bread rolls, and olives. The smell of cooked meats was sensational and they looked hungrily at the spread. Wine cups were already filled with red wine and the women collected a cup and each sat with a drink, patiently waiting for Zeus and Themis to join them.

'So,' Nemesis offered.

'So?' Dike asked.

'Lantis?' Nemesis was surprised.

'It is an original name,' offered Dike.

'I have not heard it used as a name before,' agreed Astraea.

'Did father speak of his intentions for the baby?' asked Dike.

'We did not speak of it,' replied Astraea who then proceeded to recount their observance of the wedding, their visit to the potter's, and to the blacksmiths. She described what had happened, and they laughed at the part where Zeus wielded the blacksmiths sword, but would not accept it as a gift as he already had too many.

'That sword will be worth a fortune now,' observed Dike.

She stopped speaking when Zeus and Themis finally entered the room and sat with them. Themis seemed sad and Zeus appeared solemn. The others were prudent enough not to ask. Zeus handed a cup of wine to Themis and she took a sip.

Nemesis thought it strange and that perhaps they should be proposing a toast to the birth of their son. 'Is Lantis sleeping?'

'Yes,' answered Themis.

Astraea rose and gathered food on a plate and started to eat. Dike and Nemesis followed her lead. Zeus then got himself some food and he motioned to Themis.

'I am not hungry,' she said softly.

They mostly ate in silence. After a while, Themis asked Astraea 'Did you take your father to meet Gorontalo?'

'Not yet mother,' Astraea replied.

'We spent time with the Potters' and the Blacksmiths,' Zeus added.

'Perhaps the three of you can take him to Gorontalo after you have finished eating,' Themis suggested.

'I should stay with you,' offered Dike.

'I'll be fine,' Themis assured her.

'You should eat,' suggested Zeus.

'Yes, you should,' added Nemesis. 'You need to keep your strength up.'

Themis smiled at their concern. 'I will eat something after I have rested. Lantis will want a feed soon,' she told them.

They continued eating in silence for a while, and then Zeus emptied his cup and cleared his throat. He rose and stretched. 'I am ready when you are,' he informed them.

'I want to freshen up before we go out again,' said Astraea. She got up and left the room.

'Me too,' replied Dike and she got up and followed Astraea as did Nemesis.

Now that they were alone, Themis asked Zeus, 'When shall we tell them?'

'Tomorrow night at supper I think,' he announced and then paused. 'Let me complete the tour of your island first.'

'I am tired and I am going to bed,' Themis told him.

'You do seem like you need a rest,' Zeus confirmed sympathetically. He noticed that Themis was crying. He held her and kissed her gently. 'I think I should freshen up also,' he said as he turned and left the room.

Themis walked solemnly back to her room. A servant was sitting on a chair next to where Lantis slept. Themis dismissed her and she looked over at her boy. He was noticeably larger. Her tears now flooded down her cheek and her face blushed a deep red. She threw herself onto her bed and wept until, from sheer exhaustion, she fell into a restless sleep.

***

Zeus completed his ablutions and returned to the main dining area. He found Nemesis in the seated in the room. She was resting on a couch piled with cushions. She held a cup of wine to her lips and held a roasted chicken drumstick in the other hand.

'I have to keep my strength up,' she explained saluting her father with the cup.

He poured wine for himself and then sat beside her. 'It will be your turn soon,' he said in a melodic tone.

'I am not rushing my pregnancy. I expect to go full term,' she advised him.

'Good for you,' he proclaimed.

Nemesis studied the father of her child. She had no expectations of him with her baby. She could sense that something terrible was going to happen to Lantis, and she hoped he did not have nefarious plans for her child.

Zeus looked at her and smiled broadly.

I hope he does not expect to have sex with me tonight, thought Nemesis.

'Could you do a job for me please?' Zeus asked her.

That was a strange way to ask for sex… but maybe it is not sex that he is after she mused but said nothing.

'Nemesis?'

'Of course, my lord. I was just waiting for you to tell me what it was,' she blurted.

'I am curious about these games. It seems to me that there are people doing evil. I think people are being cheated and some are being hurt.'

'Do you still want me to investigate?'

'Yes. Will you do that for me?'

'Of course, father.'

'I need you to do it today. Can you do it that quickly?'

I can make a start.'

'If there a people using these sporting events for corruption and illegal profiteering, I would like them to be tried and if it is agreed that they are guilty, then I want them to be publicly executed. We need to make an example of them,' he explained.

'I understand and I completely agree. The harmony enjoyed by the people of Thera deserves protecting,' she explained.

'Good!' he paused 'Can you start now?'

'At once, my lord,' Nemesis agreed. She got up and headed for the front door. She picked up a satchel and shouldered it. She waved at Zeus, turned and headed outside.

When Dike and Astraea entered the room, they strode up to their father and stood before Zeus in anticipation of their departure.

'I have decided that we should rest. Let us meet here in the morning and get a fresh start.

Both Dike and Astraea seemed relieved to be staying in. They nodded their agreement.

***

The following morning, they all met in the dining room. There were indications that Nemesis had eaten and had already left the palace as she was nowhere to be seen.

'She told me she had a lot of work to do,' explained Zeus when the others asked.

'I presume Nemesis is investigating the games for you. If she finds evidence of illegal activities, we will need to have a trial and prosecute them,' Astraea explained.

Themis sat with Lantis suckling at her breast. He now appeared to be the size of a two-year-old and Themis looked drained. Dike and Astraea fetched food for her and then themselves. 'I have already started him on solid foods,' she explained, 'but he seems to enjoy my breast milk, and he is such a gentleman as he is considerate and careful not to use his teeth.'

'He has teeth?'

'At least twenty from what I can see,' she reported.

'I wonder how long Nemesis will be,' pondered Dike.

'You know Nemesis, when she is focused, she will investigate every angle and find the perpetrators.'

'When we hear her report, we will prepare accordingly,' stated Themis.

Dike and Astraea nodded their agreement. They all ate hungrily and were soon contented with their bellies full of food.

'What would you like to do today, father?' asked Dike.

'I thought we could meet this medicine man that you have been referring too?' he answered.

'Gorontalo,' explained Themis. 'Yes, I think it would be good for you to meet him,' she agreed.

'Okay then, let's get going.'

'He is doing some astonishing work on disease control,' Themis added.

'I look forward to meeting him,' said Zeus.

'I must warn you, that he is a bit of an anti-god person.'

'Anti-god?' asked Zeus incredulously.

'He is one of those self-determinationalists,' contributed Dike.

'Those people seem to be growing in numbers, and they are becoming more popular here on Thera,' Zeus observed.

'They are just a fad, father. We are not concerned. The people love and need us,' Dike assured him.

'Good,' agreed Zeus standing up. 'And so, they should.'

Dike and Astraea stood up also.

Zeus walked to Themis and kissed her. Themis smiled in delighted surprise. He motioned to hold the baby.

'He is feeding!' she denied him.

'Just for a moment,' he explained. 'He can get back to feeding when we are gone.'

She pulled him off her nipple. His lips made a smacking sound as the suction was pulled free. Lantis seemed disappointed at being interrupted from his meal. Zeus chuckled.

'He is growing so fast!' he exclaimed.

'He will be big and strong, just like his father,' Themis contributed.

Zeus returned Lantis to his mother who put him onto the other breast.

'Lucky fellow,' said Zeus about his son.

Astraea and Dike returned from freshening up and they were now ready to leave.

They left the palace and were soon walking through the city. It was another magnificent sunny blue-sky day. It was warm, but not hot, and a gentle breeze refreshed the air. People gathered to them and soon they had a crowd of followers.

'See how the people love us father,' contributed Dike.

'They are probably hoping that I will throw some lightning bolts at something, or someone,' Zeus muttered.

'Father!' Dike admonished.

'Astraea, you have been quiet lately,' observed Zeus.

'I have been wondering about your plans for Lantis,' she replied.

'I will explain them to all of you tonight,' he assured her.

'And your plans for Thera?' she asked and looked at him with deep concern. 'I truly want to know.'

'Also, tonight,' he replied.

For a while they strolled in silence. Both Astraea and Dike sensed that their father would not be drawn to explain more than that. He would only explain himself when he was ready. Zeus happily walked with his two daughters down the main street of Akrotiri. He held out his arms in playful companionship, and they happily linked arms and laughed as they strolled. Their entourage cheered and hooted their support and appreciation of the happy threesome. It seemed everyone was as cheerful. They were as good as the weather and the weather was perfect.

Zeus, Astraea, and Dike arrived at Gorontalo's practice. He greeted them as soon they approached his door. He had been alerted to their arrival by all the commotion of the crowd of people who now accompanied Zeus and his daughters.

'Father, this is Gorontalo,' Astraea introduced.

'Gorontalo, this is our father, Zeus,' explained Astraea somewhat unnecessarily.

'An honour,' responded Gorontalo.

'May we visit with you inside?' asked Zeus indicating the cumbersome crowd.

'Of course, my lord,' Gorontalo stepped aside opening the door wider for them as to invite them in. The crowd moved closer and he hastily followed his guests closing the door on the multitude.

They looked about the room as their eyes adjusted to the darkness after being in bright sunlight.

'What can this humble servant do for you my lord, Zeus?' he asked them. 'Are you injured?'

'We have no injury,' Zeus replied. 'I am just curious,' he added.

'Curious, my lord?' Gorontalo asked expectantly.

'Yes.'

'May we sit, Gorontalo?' asked Dike.

'Where are my manners!' he exclaimed. 'Please, make yourself comfortable,' he offered.

He busied himself fetching bowls of water for each of his visitors and then he sat down with them.

'Please tell me about your work here,' asked Zeus.

'My lord, I am a doctor of medicine. I clean and bind wounds; I prepare balms and healing ointments to prevent infection, and I do my best to cure disease,' he explained.

'And?' invited Zeus.

'I also own and manage a school of medicine,' added Gorontalo. 'Some pay me to learn, and others are apprenticed. I do my best to train others in the arts of medicine so that more people can become healers.'

'I hear that you are doing a fantastic job on both accounts,' praised Zeus.

Thank you, my lord,' responded Gorontalo. 'I am gratified to be acknowledged by you in this way.'

'Please, tell me more,' invited Zeus once more.

Gorontalo was proud of his work and was delighted to have such a powerful audience. Perhaps he had misjudged this god. Maybe there was hope for respectable working relationships between humans and the gods after all.

'Before medicines and healing became popular, sick and injured people turned to the gods to heal them,' he explained. 'Often their natural immunities would be enough to heal them, but when they died, everyone readily agreed that it was simply the will of the gods.'

Zeus nodded encouragingly.

Gorontalo continued. 'I became suspicious of the gods' interventions for them and I saw no evidence of it. I concluded that we would be better off fending for ourselves, using human medical treatments to care for sick humans. Now medical practitioners readily assist the sick and injured thereby reducing their suffering and decreasing the mortality rate. As a result of medicine and treatment, we now rely on the gods for fewer things.' Gorontalo was enjoying himself. He was fulfilling his fantasy of "Telling it how it is" to the highest god of all the lands.

'Previously, infant mortality was so high, that one in three babies were dying before their first birthday. Are these deaths "the will of the gods"?' he asked rhetorically.

Zeus said nothing.

'Keeping your wife pure is also significant form of disease control. If a wife or daughter is violated or molested by another man, she may have contracted a sexually transmitted disease which can then pass on to her husband or future husband,' he explained, speaking rapidly and in great excitement. He felt that Zeus silence was an acknowledgment of what he spoke about and that he, Zeus both understood and agreed.

He continued, 'Common thinking was that only woman could have the disease and that they would pass it onto a men. Men believed that they could not give to sickness to woman. A woman's purity was therefore highly valued. Her faithfulness was paramount so as to remove the husband's risk of contracting the dreaded disease. In reality, it did not stop men from having sex with other women, but it did isolate the wife. Because of this belief, many women lost their right to participate in the affairs of the community, trade, own property, education, and were forced to live a life of isolation and total subservience and obedience to their man.'

He was on a roll now. but he paused a moment to let all that sink in. 'But!' he then exclaimed. 'It is not true.'

'Not true?' asked Zeus confused.

'No!' Men can give the disease to woman just as easily as men give it to women. The male subjugation of women is therefore utterly unnecessary,' he explained excitedly.

Zeus looked at him blankly.

'Monogamy is the best form of sexual disease control,' explained Gorontalo.

'Monogamy! Well, that might work with humans but....'

'And now medicines!' declared Gorontalo. 'I am experimenting with medicines which show much promise in curing both men and woman of the diseases contracted through sexual intercourse!'

'That, is impressive,' conceded Zeus and he nodded knowingly.

'So, you see, we will not be calling on the gods to heal us,' he scoffed teasingly. 'We will now heal ourselves.'

'You openly mock the works of Apollo and Asclepius?' Zeus said in an astounded voice.

'I only challenge the ancient custom that we should surrender the solution to our medical problems to the mercy of the gods. We must practice medicine and keep learning to get better at it. We have a prevailing duty to care for the sick and injured.'

'But you will still need us for spiritual guidance and law and order?' said Astraea and she seemed astonished about his medical opinions.

'We can police and judge ourselves also,' countered Gorontalo. 'We can appoint public servants to manage community matters, and we raise taxes to pay for them. The people will gladly pay them as they will be used for the mutual benefit of all citizens,' he added.

Zeus said nothing.

'But you need us,' Astraea was almost pleading. She could feel a swell of teardrops forming in her eyes.

Dike stood up, 'Father, have you heard enough?'

Zeus also stood. He took Gorontalo's hand and shook it. 'You are doing great work with healing the sick and injured,' he told him. 'You have some interesting propositions that I will now deliberate on.'

'Thank you,' replied Gorontalo gratefully. He was pleased that he had expressed his views.

'But I suggest you keep out of politics and law,' Zeus told him sternly. Humans are corruptible, and it will not do to have you managing each other without us to rule and guide you.'

'But...' stammered Gorontalo.

'Without us, the strong will intentionally hurt weaker humans. They will lie, and cheat, and wrongfully imprison other people. They will mistreat, kill, enslave... you name it, a human will find a way to decry others for their own malicious benefit.'

'That's not fair,' Gorontalo was aghast. 'Humans are fundamentally caring and nurturing towards each other.'

'No, sadly that is not true. Humans have the greatest capacity for cruelties from all living things. I have seen much evidence of this. It is the fear of the god's wrath that keeps human behaviour in check. You just stick to your medicine and healing, and we will get along fine.'

'And if I don't?' defied Gorontalo.

'Then you will die, and it will be soon,' Zeus explained matter-of-factly.

Zeus turned and headed out of the building closely followed by Astraea and Dike. They adjusted to the bright sunlight. Their entourage had now dwindled. 'Where to now?' he asked the two women.

***

Zeus, Astraea, and Dike left the healer and walked through the streets in a subdued silence. They came across a theatre. Actors were working through their lines under the direction of the lead actor.

They were invited to sit and watch.

Astraea and Dike were only too pleased when their father accepted the invitation. They needed a calming distraction after their confrontation with the healer.

On Thera, attending the theatre was a popular pastime, and audiences equally enjoyed the dramas and the comedies. They were the first actors to write down their lines, and in this way, they would be able to repeat their tried and tested plays before a new audience. Successful actors and writers were encouraged with financial rewards and other accolades. Yet, impromptu comedic entertainers were still popular, as were street performers who would juggle, mime, or sing raunchy ballads.

Most plays were performed by three actors who played all the parts. When needed, a crane was used hoist the actor to simulate the flying god or goddess. Satirical plays that mocked the gods and goddesses were especially popular. The producers or Choregoi, were responsible for organising singers, dancers, and musicians. They funded the theatre and after covering costs, they divided any remaining profits.

The lead actor approached Zeus and asked 'Would you like a song my lord?'

Zeus nodded his agreement.

The Choregos waved his hands and a chorus of performers came dancing onto the stage. They clapped in unison and began singing. They appropriately sang a song of praise of the gods that was popular among humans during the good times.

Dike and Astraea beamed in happiness. This was the much-needed reassurance that these goddesses hoped that Zeus would like to hear.

The three applauded their appreciation and then got up to leave the performance area.

***

They met with some merchants. They proudly showed Zeus new coins that were being introduced into the trading houses. These coins were embossed with numbers that multiplied their original value proportionately to the number.

Coins with denominations on them had revolutionised trade. The merchants were beside themselves with this concept of portable wealth. The valued coins were minted from precious metals such as gold, silver, and bronze. They all spoke of them as being "the way of the future".

'This is Plouto's doing,' explained Astraea to her father.

'Do you think they will catch on?' asked Zeus incredulously holding up a bronze coin with a ten stamped on it, and a silver coin that was embossed with a symbol representing one hundred.

'The Egyptian merchants are agreed that they will embrace this innovation. They say they are now committed to this form of value exchange,' explained one of the merchants.

'Do you do much with the Egyptian traders?' Zeus asked.

'Not yet. Trade with them is still only emerging.'

'What about Sparta?' he asked.

'Not so much my lord. They are a bit backward on the mainland,' he explained. 'They only trust the metal and not the number we have minted on them.'

They excitedly spoke about new products and offered samples to Zeus and his daughters.

***

Cattle were native animals to Greece and the Greeks were quick to realise their value for dairy and meat. They domesticated them and farmed them with great care and skill. Merchants sold both meat and dairy products. Even their waste was prized, though at a much lower value.

Olive oil production began in earnest when the farmers discovered the many uses for it. They extracted the oil by crushing the fruit with a stone roller. They would ladle the fruit into finely woven sacks which were placed on a flat table with raised edges. A stone plate, mounted under a beam was used to press down on the olives. Then hot water was poured onto the sacks and the fruit pressed once more. This process was repeated several times, and the oil and water were directed to drain into urns. The oil, being lighter than water, floats to the top. The olive oil is then skimmed off using a ladle. The remaining flesh trapped inside the sacks is discarded. The sacks are then washed for reuse. Olive trees were soon so highly prized that it became a serious offence to harm or uproot one.

An olive oil merchant approached them. He bowed respectfully. 'I want to gift to you my olive oil,' he said giving it to Astraea.

She took the proffered urn. 'Thank you, but we already have plenty of olive oil,' she told him.

'But my oil is exceptional, and highly prized,' the merchant explained.

'How so?' asked Zeus.

'I have perfected a filter to vastly improve the clarity and purity of the oil,' he explained.

Zeus looked at him.

'My oil is extra pure. I call it extra virgin olive oil,' he explained as he smiled at Astraea.

'Extra Virgin?' asked Zeus. 'That is an interesting term for it,' he added. He smiled at Dike and Astraea. Astraea was not smiling, but Dike could see the humour in it, and she politely turned her grinning face away from Astraea.

'I would like to name my olive oil after you as "Astraea's extra virgin olive oil" in your honour,' he explained to Astraea.

Astraea looked horrified.

Zeus roared in laughter. Dike also thought it funny, but when she saw the horror in Astraea's face, she sided with her sister and comforted her. She gave Zeus her look of admonishment and Zeus quietened.

Astraea was aggrieved, 'You will not, not now or ever, name your oil after me!' she screeched at the befuddled man. The merchant's face turned a lighter shade of pale. 'And if you dare to insult me this way again, I will hunt you down and pour your own boiling hot oil down your throat! Do you understand me!' she screamed.

'Yes! A thousand apologies, yes!' The merchant spluttered and was clearly in shock at her response. His face was turned as pale as bleached linen.

'I think he meant it as an honour to you, my dear,' offered Zeus.

'Well, clearly he failed,' declared Astraea and she stormed off.

'My lord,' stammered the olive merchant. 'She is the goddess of growing olives, is she not?'

'What?' Dike seemed confused.

'She is Aristaeus…' mumbled the merchant. 'The cultivator of olive trees and their harvest…'

'Her name is Astraea, and she is known as the goddess of purity, innocence, and justice, you idiot!' she explained to at him unkindly.

Zeus roared with laughter at the merchant's mistaken identity. He regained his composure sufficiently to add, 'But she certainly is a virgin,' Zeus explained and laughed at the olive oil merchant some more.

Dike ran after her sister to explain the merchant's mistake.

Zeus studied the merchant and then chuckled once more. The merchant now backed away, fearful that Zeus would hurt him. Zeus simply turned and followed his daughters, hastening to catch up with them and he was still chuckling as he walked.

***

Zeus, Astraea, and Dike passed another wedding feast similar to the wedding that they witnessed earlier. They were invited to have a drink and share some of the wonderful food on offer.

Thirsty and hungry, the three politely accepted the invitation. But they would only stay for a short while as they did not want to interrupt the festivities.

Wine was regularly consumed by men during feasting. At formal gatherings the only woman permitted during the revelry were singers, dancers, and fornicators. On this occasion, being a wedding, the bride and her friends were also present.

The bride's parents came to meet Zeus. 'My lord, you humble us with your appearance. Your presence is a good omen for my daughter and her husband.'

'We are delighted to be included in your celebration,' Zeus replied modestly.

The man sat close to them for a while, enjoying the familiarity. He turned to Zeus and spoke in a hushed voice. 'My lord, do you see those two men over there by that large black urn?' he asked him.

He looked. 'Yes,' Zeus acknowledged.

'Observe the fun,' he invited. 'The older man is with the young groom that will soon marry his daughter. The father is getting him intoxicated, and he will soon offer him a forbidden temptation to test his metal.'

The younger man spilled some wine down his shirt and he roared in laughter at the humour of it. The elder man laughed also, and there was mutual back slapping. As they watched, the elder man summoned a young, scantily clad, but physically mature woman to where they sat. He invited her to sit on the groom's lap. The woman raised her skirts and made to sit down on him, but he fended her off. The younger man laughed again but nervously this time. The woman jumped on his lap and so he stood up forcing her to her feet.

Clearly, the young man was confused by his future father in laws scandalous invitation. The girl was exceptionally pretty and very alluring, but he made the decision not to accept her. He stood somewhat wobbly on his feet, he bowed to girl and his future father-in-law, offered his polite apologies, and ran away from the area.

All the men, including their host, burst into laughter.

'He will now be allowed to marry his daughter,' their host explained.

'He was testing him?' queried Astraea.

'It is better to find out what kind of man he is, before he gives him his daughter,' explained their host.

'We should leave,' Zeus decided. 'Thank you for your hospitality and for the entertainment.'

'We have a saying, "After three bowls of wine, wise guests know to go home",' explained their host. 'But you only have had one.'

Zeus stood. 'Thank you, but we are intruders not guests,' he explained. 'Besides, we have much to do.'

The host showed his disappointment, but he indicated with a nod that he understood.

They left and headed for the palace.

Ploutos confronted them as they walked toward the palace. He was swaying and Zeus and Astraea approached him to see what was wrong. 'Ploutos. What is wrong with you?' she asked.

'Exactly! What is wrong with me?' he slurred his words.

'By Dionysus, he is drunk' Zeus observed.

'I love you so much,' Ploutos drawled.

'But I hardly know you nephew' Zeus replied kindly.

'No, no, no, no, no … not you, uncle.' he explained as he turned and pointed at Astraea. 'Her!' he declared still swaying.

Zeus turned to ask Astraea. 'Are you certain that you do not share this man's passion?'

'No father. I would go as far as stating that I do not like him at all, and I particularly do not approve of his drinking, or off his profiteering values.'

Zeus put his hand on Ploutos neck and squeezed. It was gentle at first.

'Get some sleep, Ploutos,' he told him. He squeezed hard and Ploutos fell into a faint and landed heavily on the ground. Zeus did nothing to ease his fall.

'That will add to his hangover,' Zeus informed Astraea smiling.

'Do we move him?' she asked with scant concern.

'Let him sleep it off,' Zeus recommended. 'He probably will not remember anything in the morning anyhow.'

They left Ploutos on the ground and headed for the palace once more.

***

When they returned to see Themis and Lantis at the Palace they discovered that he was much bigger. His growth was remarkable, and he now walked and behaved like a six-year-old. He delighted them by calling them by their names when they arrived, and he quickly formed an attachment to Astraea and wanted to sit on her lap. Astraea was still fuming about the olive merchant, and Ploutos behaviour, and so she delighted in the warmth and love expressed by the little boy's obvious affection for her. She did not understand his fondness for her, but went she with along with it and she immediately she felt better.

Nemesis had returned from investigating the happenings at the games. They sat at the table, enjoying a light meal while she reported what she learned. She was able to confirm that there was corruption and race fixing. Gambling was encouraged and many families had unduly suffered because the men had made improper bets when the backer already knew the predetermined outcome. She was incensed and they agreed that the perpetrators would be prosecuted and punished.

Later that evening, in hushed tones, Zeus then outlined his plans for Lantis and the people of Thera. 'The Theran's have progressed much, and you are to be commended for the amazing work that you have done with them. But in doing so, they have become too independent from us. I need all humans to revere and worship us without hesitation. Human worship of their gods is what maintains us, and without that, we will have no place or purpose. To this end, we must destroy all Theran's...'

'No!' Themis blurted. 'These are good people. They deserve better. They have not done anything wrong and they should not be punished for our introduction of progressive thinking...' Themis was now sobbing uncontrollably. She collapsed into Nemesis's arms.

'Father.' Astraea now looked sternly at Zeus. 'There must be a better way.'

The women were clearly saddened by his decision, but he would not change it. Finally he said softly. 'I will find a way to spare as many lives as I can, but this society and all that it stands for, will end. I am concerned about the military response to all of this when they realise what is happening.'

Dike spoke up 'Tomorrow, I will take you to meet the military commander and we will make sure that he understands what is expected of him.'

Zeus nodded his appreciation.

After much talk and plenty of sobbing, they all finally retired to their bed chambers to rest, but none of the women slept much that night.

***

After they breakfasted, Zeus and Dike headed off to meet with the military commander. 'Military service has always been highly regarded,' explained Zeus to Dike as they walked.

Dike said nothing. She was content to listen to her father's explanation.

'They protect the township and the people from theft, banditry, and from invasion from neighbouring villages or kingdoms,' he added. 'Often, a well-planned defence makes all the difference in a hostile attack. More importantly, for most warriors it is a rite of passage into manliness. Later in life, as a proven man they will have earned the right to participate in politics.'

'I doubt that our politicians have ever served in the military,' Dike observed. 'We do not have the need for much in the way of a military presence on this island.

'It is a problem that we will have to remedy,' concluded Zeus. 'I need many men in uniform to assist me with what we are about to achieve.'

'Do military men get paid?' Dike asked.

'Only if they don't die,' he smirked. 'Generally, they do earn coin. Also, a soldier gets the right to acquire wealth through invasion by reaping the spoils of plunder,' he explained. 'Sometimes, that is the only reward they will ever earn, but often it is enough to satisfy desperate men.'

Zeus and Dike were greeted by the guards at the military commanders' home. They were expediently taken to meet him.

'Commander Acrisius at your service,' he announced as he stood erect and saluted.

'I am Zeus, and this is my daughter Dike,' Zeus introduced them both.

'You are both well known, my lord,' Acrisius confirmed.

'Good,' responded Zeus smiling at Dike. 'We have several matters to discuss with you Acrisius,' Zeus informed him.

'How may I be of service?' he replied to Zeus.

'Do not ask me to explain how I know, but please accept that I do,' Zeus told him.

Acrisius stared at Zeus, but he said nothing.

'These islands will soon be devastated by an enormous explosion. You homes will soon cease to exist,' Zeus announced and then watched for his reaction.

The commander turned pale. 'Do we have enough time to evacuate everyone?' he asked.

'Yes,' Zeus assured him. 'There should be enough time to get all of the people off the island, and they should depart for other lands to start a fresh life. I have contracted many seafaring merchants to provide their ships for this purpose.'

'Our people will not be betrayed and sold into slavery?' the commander asked and was clearly concerned.

'No. I would learn of it, but I promise you that will not happen,' he explained to Acrisius. 'Those merchants will be well paid to transport you all to safety.'

Acrisius said nothing.

'Each passenger will be given a written pass to show the officials when they arrive at the port that they are to be well treated or they will suffer the wrath of all the gods,' Zeus explained.

'Where are these pass ports?' he asked.

'They are being prepared and will be ready when the first ships arrive,' Zeus informed him.

Acrisius nodded his understanding.

'Also, there is to be a trial,' Zeus advised him.

'A trial my lord?'

'There is evidence of corruption, illegal gambling, cheating, bribery, and threats of death in relation to the sporting games that have become popular on the island,' Zeus informed him.

'Some of my men have competed in these games,' explained the commander.

'And what was their experience?' Dike asked.

'They felt aggrieved, cheated, and generally disappointed with the results. My men train hard and they are physically fit. They can run fast. They have often lost a race when it would seem improbable for them to do so. How can we assist you?' asked Acrisius.

'Two-fold,' answered Zeus. 'Firstly, we expect a protest from the citizens. Not about the reasons for the trial as we believe that most people already believe they know the verdict, but there are some people who feel that mortals should be tried by mortals and without the judgement of the Gods. They may interfere with the process.'

'No!' Acrisius was clearly shocked. 'There would be much more corruption if that was to happen.'

'Our system works, because we goddesses have nothing to personally to gain from favouring one human over another,' Dike contributed.

'Secondly, these crimes are severe. Once found guilty I will need your men to execute the sentences.'

'It will be done my lord,' Acrisius saluted.

'There is one additional item,' said Zeus.

'My lord?'

'Each person leaving Thera must drink water before they are allowed to board their ship.'

'My lord?'

'This water is special. It has an herbal component to it that will allow everyone to relax and keep calm, despite having to deal with the stress of an evacuation,' Zeus explained.

'They will be distraught,' added Dike. 'They are losing their homes, livelihoods, memories...'

'The enhanced water will be ready by the time the first ships arrive,' Zeus informed him.

'I understand,' confirmed Acrisius. 'It will be administered to every man, woman, and child before they board the vessels,' he assured them.

***

The following day, Astraea was absent. She was busy researching the prosecution's case against the people accused of the crimes committed during the games.

Themis, Dike and Nemesis were also busy preparing for the trial.

Zeus meanwhile, visited the markets, community centres, and schools. He sought out vantage points and summoned crowds of people to come to him and he resonantly told the people of Thera about their impending evacuation. They respectfully gathered to hear his announcements. 'The people of Thera, gather your families, and prized possessions, and prepare to depart Thera. This island and the islands close by, will soon be consumed by forces of nature that I cannot tame. Your homes will cease to exist. You must spread my words to every person, and be prepared to evacuate Thera within ten days. Ships have been organised to save you all and they will transport you to new lands to continue your lives.'

His news was received with stunned disbelief. It was Zeus's pronouncement and so no one would deny its validity, but still it was difficult to accept that their homes would be destroyed and that they had to leave before the disaster struck.

Zeus also enlisted the leaders and officials that he met, and he ordered them to continue the message of the need for everyone to get ready to depart.

When he returned to the palace, he discovered that Lantis was now the size of a twelve-year-old! He rushed into his father's welcoming embrace. Zeus was now feeling a little guilty for his son's fate, but what had been set into motion, could no longer be avoided.

***

The following week the trial against a family accused of crimes of cheating at the games was being held. The charges also included the criminal use of intimidation, threats of violence, actual harm to other individuals, and for bringing the sporting events into disrepute.

Themis had distanced herself from Astraea and Nemesis, who were finalising their argument for bringing these accused persons before the court.

Only Dike had remained to assist her. Together they had discussed the charges, reviewed customs and precedents, and they had prepared the room for the court trial. Themis hoped that it would all be resolved in one day.

The goddess Adikia had been invited to the island by Zeus who believed that the defendants, despite the overwhelming evidence against them, should have representation and Adikia was his obvious choice to do so. Adika was the goddess of injustice and criminal behaviour.

Eris had also turned up with her. She was the goddess of discord and strife and she was often in Adikia's company. Together, they had arrived on the island and they were now busily preparing a defence for the accused.

Initially, Themis was incensed that Zeus had invited these two undesirable goddesses to the island to defend these people. She argued that the people would be given a fair trial as due process was being followed. The evidence against them would be proved and they would be convicted.

Zeus dismissed her objections and argued that Advika and Eris would test the process, argue the charges, and perhaps discover ways and means of mitigating the severity of crimes. He explained that when the final result was reached, that everyone would be satisfied that all aspects had been taken into account, and that the verdict would be beyond any doubt.

Themis capitulated to his reasoning, but she made it clear that she did not like Advika or Eris.

Zeus told her that her feelings toward them were irrelevant.

So, Themis now focused on the trial with thoughts about the need for impartiality in making a judgment that was purely based on the evidence submitted and the defence presented. She reluctantly decided that she could not achieve this with clear impartiality, so she decided to recruit twelve citizens that were unconnected with the trial or the accused, and allow the prosecutors and defence counsellors to prove or disprove the charges to them. She would preside to ensure that the due process was followed, but she would remain impartial to the outcome. This trial was becoming more relevant to the future of court hearings and justice for all humankind. Themis hoped that the new processoers of justice that they were achieving here today would survive the evacuation of the islanders and the destruction of Thera.

***

Advika relished the opportunity to work against Dike. The two had a long-standing hatred for each other and were often depicted as being at odds. Artisans would depict them on murals and vases with Dike as the young vibrant defender of justice, and Advika was depicted as an old crone of a woman who as the advocate of injustice as being punished in the popular depiction of good defeating evil. In truth, Advika was a stunningly beautiful goddess as was Eris. In the past, when they were defending the accused, they would often reference those occasions where the innocent was wrongfully accused and part of her role was to expose the weaknesses of the prosecutors' arguments.

Advika best displayed her strengths in an adversarial verbal contest such as a court room, however this was the first time she had defended humans in a trial. She and Eris normally only defended other gods and goddesses from the wrath of the council of gods at Mount Olympus.

On the mainland, it was becoming increasingly popular among miscreants to invoke Advika and Eris to advocate on their behalf when they being prosecuted for a crime.

Advika had insisted that all prisoners be given every opportunity to prove their innocence, or at a minimum be able to mitigate the severity of the allegations against them. Over the past week, she and Eris had spent much time with the accused family. Though they were imprisoned, she had learned as much of the truth that they were willing to share with them. They now believed they knew the truth about their activities, and they were impressed by them, but in fairness to the accused and in respect for their confidences, she would only present positive arguments that favoured the family and their innocence.

Now that it came to the start of the trial, Astraea intentionally stood close to them. She wanted to get a sense of how they were feeling. In her experience, the guilty always appeared ashamed and downcast. They were often defeated before they were tried. Their body language belied their guilt.

This family looked at Adikia for guidance and comfort. Astraea thought it was ironic that they were trying to appear indignant as they were being called to account for their criminal behaviour. She figured that Advika and Eris had told them to behave this way.

The guards led the four accused people into a holding pen within the court room. An elderly woman and three younger men were brought before Themis to be tried for crimes against the people of Thera.

She knew the woman to be the mother of the three sons who were now standing pensively before her. They were known as the "Fia's Family," and they had been charged by Nemesis of crimes for which they must now account for.

Themis had to clear the court of all citizens except for those that formed the jury. The other people were too noisy. Ironically, they were not angry about the trial of the accused. It seemed that they all felt that they were guilty, and they readily agreed with the need to bring them to trial. But they were protesting the process. Many humans believed that the fate of any humans accused of a crime should be determined by their peers and not by the gods.

Themis had reluctantly capitulated to their right to protest, but she was determined that it would not interfere with today's proceedings. So, she had the protestors forcibly removed.

Zeus watched in passive silence throughout the proceedings. Themis was quite proud of his behaviour and his decision to remain calm, despite the fact that she knew that he had been seething and indignant at the human's audacity to question the gods right to rule over people, and the god's role in being judgemental over them. As Zeus knew the fate of these humans, it was easy for him to let their errant behaviour pass.

Even with the protestors removed outside, they could still hear their angry voices.

Zeus had never come across this type of behaviour before in any of the regions that he ruled, or in any of the other places that he had frequented.

Zeus was previously concerned that once it was widely known that the people of Thera had absolute self-determination, then that ideology would spread to other lands. He believed strongly that the god's right to rule over humans must never be challenged. He was pleased that his solution for Thera would eliminate this threat. His thoughts were interrupted by Themis.

Themis called out, 'Astraea, would you state your case against the defendants please?'

Astraea stood before the Court and spoke in a calm and even voice. 'I have discovered that the accused are guilty of corruption in relation to the games, competitions, and other festivals held on the island of Thera. Today, I shall prove these charges to the court.' She let the words sink in before she continued. 'These four people have manipulated the results of races through race fixing, bribery, and threats of violence's against officials and competitors.'

'To what end?' asked Themis.

'In order to unfairly profit from the result when wagering with gamblers on an outcome that they had predetermined,' she replied. 'Those people placing bets never had any chance of winning. They were deceived and cheated.'

'Do you have witnesses?' Themis asked.

'I call, Hesiod to speak before the court!' she called out briskly.

Hesiod stood up.

'Please Hesiod. In your own words, share with the court what you have told me,' Astraea invited.

'Well...' Hesiod hesitated. He glanced at the four accused uncertainly.

'Hesiod, are you guilty of a crime?' Themis asked him.

'No!' he recoiled in shock.

'Then you have nothing to fear in telling us the truth.'

He glanced at the accused again and then nodded his capitulation. 'You see... we have been arranging the games for about four years now,' he began. 'In the beginning there were only seven events, that has now grown to twenty. Each region selects their champions to represent them in the events. In that way the honour of winning goes to both the competitor and the region that sponsors them.' He then turned toward Astraea for support.

She nodded her encouragement and motioned for him to elaborate.

So, he continued. 'Last year, several strangers appeared claiming that they were representing their regions. At first, we did not think much of it, but these athletes were exceptionally fast and they won most of the prizes. They were properly registered to compete, but we had never seen any of these athletes before.'

'Did you think that strange?'

'Yes! We know who is who at our games. We know all about the promising young competitors who are training to take on the resident champions. But we did not recognise who these new people were. They were not from Thera, but they were being sponsored by Theran's. We did not say anything last year, but we thought it unfair on the Theran's that had trained so hard only to be beaten by athletes who we believe are from the mainlands.' He looked down as he paused.

He then stared at the accused. In a loud voice he explained. 'Those four were the instigators of the arrival of new competitors. We learned that they had sought out fast runners, champion boxers, wrestlers, and archers from other lands that could be temporarily adopted by the "Fia's Family" on Thera and then compete in their name. They knew that they would win, so that when they gambled on the outcome, they already knew the result, and they had an illegal and immoral advantage over the punters. We call that cheating!'

'How could you possibly know that they would win?' asked Advika. 'Would it be fair to say that each competitor had an equal chance of winning in a properly staged event? That the outcome was based on their speed or strength, or perhaps on their personal determination to win?'

'They did know the outcome. They always knew the result before it happened,' replied Hesiod, 'Because they intimidated the other competitors into losing.'

'How was that achieved?' asked Astraea.

'They threatened the other competitors with injury, or to their family members, if they dared win the event.'

'Did they ever carry out these threats?' asked Astraea.

Hesiod looked down again. 'Yes,' he mumbled. 'On many occasions.'

'Tell us about them,' invited Themis.

'Ma Fia and her sons burnt down the house of 'Jusco. Jusco won the first foot race this year. His wife and three children died in that fire.'

'That's not true!' yelled one of the accused men.

'I caught you doing it,' a man claimed from the back of the court room.

'No interruptions please,' Themis admonished.

'If it pleases the court, this man is my next witness,' Astraea explained.

The man stood up and walked to the front and stood beside Astraea. 'My name is Jusco,' he said as he introduced himself and then he pointed. 'Those people killed my family because I won that stupid race.'

'I rest my case,' Astraea declared and sat down hiding a grin.

'Dike. Is there any precedent or custom that we should be aware of?'

Dike stood up.

'These events or "games" as they are called, are a relatively new feature within our culture, so there is no precedent as such. However, in all competitions, there is always a community sense of equal opportunity when competing to win. Cheating has always been actively discouraged. Therefore, cheating causing injury or death is always punished by equal measure,' she explained and then sat down.

'Thank you,' said Themis.

Then looking at Advika she asked. 'Advika. In your dealing with those charged of murder and of corruption, have you found any thing you'd like to present that may explain or excuse their behaviour?' asked Themis.

Advika stood and stepped up to the accused in the holding pen. 'Ma Fia, Roscoe, Penda, and Dieter were somewhat influenced in their greed by us, their gods, my lady Themis.'

'Please explain,' Themis invited.

Zeus was now interested and he sat upright as he audibly cleared his throat.

Advika now realised that she was on dangerous ground. Any attack on the gods was criticism of Zeus. Her words could be construed as a rebuke of her king. So, Advika decided she would pick her words carefully. 'Ploutos is the son of Demeter...' she started to explain.

'We know who Ploutos is, Advika,' Themis said now looking at Zeus. She too was concerned where Advika was taking her line of argument.

Advika paused in thought. She had concluded the guilt of the four accused, but she still felt compelled to speak in their favour. She also did not like to fight what was clearly losing argument.

'Ploutos has introduced the concept of portable wealth to the humans. By introducing numbered coins, people no longer gamble for mere ducks, chickens, or pigs. People now gamble for bits of overvalued metal. As long as everyone agrees they have value, then people will want to have more of them. The minting of these coins by the gods has corrupted the humans.'

'Are you claiming Ploutos introduced coins for the purposes of gambling?' demanded Zeus.

'I am simply explaining that because of these value added coins, it is more tempting to gamble. It make these events more open to corruption, and more likely that people will manipulate the outcome as the profits of gambling increase the motive.'

'Your point is taken, thank you Advika,' Themis acknowledged and then motioned Advika to sit and she did so, understanding that her moment was over.

'I now call on the independent citizens who are our jury to these proceedings, to confer among themselves and reach an opinion.

They murmured among themselves and were now nodding their agreement. The main person signalled to Themis that they were ready.

'What say you?' Themis directed her question to the main person who everyone agreed that he would speak for them as a group.

The man stood up and received nods from people in the room. He turned to face Themis and spoke in a clear voice. 'We agree that they did these crimes and are guilty. They should be punished.' He sat down and stared at the four defendants. They appeared deflated by the outcome.

'Thank you for your time and consideration of these proceedings. You are excused,' Themis said as she dismissed the group.

Dike and Nemesis motioned for the people to get up and exit the building and they calmly did so, evidently relieved that the trial was over.

When calm had returned, she spoke again, 'It is the conclusion of this court that you four are guilty of murder and corruption,' she stated. 'Ma Fia. You and your three sons are to be savagely wounded and then fed to the pigs.'

Zeus seemed pleased. This was exactly outcome that he and Themis had agreed too.

Eight guards and their captain marched into the room. They collected the four prisoners and escorted them outside. The protestors were now hushed. They had heard the verdict and had ceased being noisy.

The guards escorted them into a covered wagon and it immediately set off to the piggery. Their sentence was duly carried out and the people of Thera now understood the fate of convicted murderers and cheats.

Zeus felt the fear of the gods rise in the people who surrounded him. He was pleased as this was the result that he wanted.

After they had returned to the palace, Zeus turned and spoke casually to Themis. 'I was impressed by the way you managed the trial.'

Thank you, Zeus. That means a lot to me,' Themis replied.

'We can utilise these enhancements to the justice process during our trials held at Mount Olympus.'

Themis heart felt saddened. She realised that Zeus had no intention of improving the criminal justice system for the humans.

***

The following day Zeus had a meeting with Themis.

'I have invited Mneme to Thera,' he advised her.

'Oh,' she replied uncertain of why he would do so.

'She will assist with the evacuation of the islands,' he added.

'I am sorry, but I do not understand,' Themis told him.

'She has large quantities of waters from the river Lethe with her.'

Themis now understood. Mneme was the goddess of memory and the river Lethe was the river of forgetfulness. 'You want the people to drink the water?' she asked him.

'It is a condition that they do so, before they can leave the island,' Zeus explained.

'They can choose?

'Yes. They can drink the water and forget about their lives on this island. They will live a new life in distant land with the opportunity for a long and prosperous life. Or they can refuse, and die here on the island.'

'So be it,' she concluded. Their capitulation was a forgone conclusion.

***

Astraea and Lantis went walking through a field adjacent to an apple orchard. Although he was only ten days old, he now had the appearance of a fifteen-year-old. His growth, motor skills, and mental acuity were developing at a phenomenal rate.

'I believe I can actually see you growing,' said Astraea clearly amazed.

'Don't all children grow as fast me?' asked Lantis.

'Er, no!' replied Astraea smiling.

'How long does it take for normal children to grow to be my size?' he asked.

'You appear to be almost an adult to me,' explained Astraea. 'For a human it would take about fifteen years, and for a god it would take many months.'

'What is a year?'

'You know how long a day is?'

'Yes.'

'There are 365 of them to a year.'

'And I am now ten of these 365 days?'

'Yes.'

'Humans grow slowly,' he concluded.

'Yes, they do,' confirmed Astraea. 'Most gods and goddesses grow quickly, but none as fast as you do.'

'Am I a god?'

'You are. You are the god of this island. Our father is the king of all the gods and the goddesses.'

'Our father is Zeus,' he stated.

'That is right.'

'Our mother is Themis.'

'That is correct also,' she confirmed.

'Is she a god?'

'Our mother is a Titaness. She is an earlier type of a goddess,' corrected Astraea.

'Goddesses have a role in human lives. What is Themis's role?' he asked.

'She is the balance in justice,' answered Astraea.

'What does that mean?'

'She hears all sides of a problem. She then gives those sides a value and decides which has more weight in an argument. She is much like a weighing scale. At first, she starts off evenly balanced, but as she hears the evidence, she decides who has the strongest position and her scales tip in their favour,' she explained.

Lantis said nothing and Astraea was becoming concerned that it may have been too much information for the boy to deal with.

'I understand,' Lantis confirmed nodding.

'I am impressed that you do.'

'I am a god. It should not surprise you too much,' he told her with a smile.

'You are right again,' she smiled. 'But... it does actually surprise me.'

'What is your role?' he asked her.

'I promote justice. My role is to prosecute the guilty while protecting the innocent from being falsely blamed for an action or an inaction,' she explained.

'Does that happen often,' he asked wanting to understand.

'Unfortunately, many people, and most of the gods, lie to protect themselves from punishment from their deviant behaviour,' she lamented.

'So, you protect the innocent?'

'I try to,' she responded.

'What is my role?' he asked her.

'Our father will explain that to you.'

'Do you know what it is?'

'I do.'

'Why don't you tell me?'

'Because father asked me not to, and I always respect father's wishes.'

'I do too,' he told her.

Astraea was relieved. 'Do you like apples?' she asked him.

'What are apples?' Lantis was now curious.

'Fruit! They grow on trees called Apple trees.'

She walked to the tree and selected a beautiful red apple. She pulled it from the tree, smelt it, approved, and then gave it to Lantis.

He took it and smelt it also.

'Bite into it,' she told him.

He looked at her doubtfully.

'It is uniquely tasty,' she assured him.

He bit into the apple and smiled in surprise. 'I like apples,' he announced.

'Good,' she said. 'So do I.' She picked herself an apple and bit into it also.

They sat in the shade and watched the people as they ate the apples. After a moment, Astraea realised that she had not explained everything to him. 'You do not eat the middle bit.'

'Oh,' replied Lantis. 'I thought I had too. It was a bit unpleasant,'

'Well, you do not have to eat it,' she explained restraining a smile.

'May I have another?' he asked.

'Have as many as you would like,' invited Astraea.

Lantis ate seven apples and Astraea thought he had better stop, or he would get a stomach ache.

'I was hungry,' he declared. He smiled and then burped.

'I am not surprised,' said Astraea laughing. 'You have been growing as I watched you. You now appear to be a fully grown adult.' she declared.

Lantis continued to grow. Astraea decided it was time to return to their home and feed him a proper meal. They walked in silence for a while and then Lantis asked her a question.

'Are you, my wife?'

'No, I am your sister,' she replied.

'Sister?' he asked confused.

'Yes, I am female and we have the same parents. Therefore, I am your sister,' she explained.

'I understand,' he told her.

'Can I marry my sister?' he asked.

'Why would you want to do that?' she asked surprised by his question.

'So that we can make a baby together, like my father and mother made me,' he explained.

'That is sweet,' she told him. 'I am a vowed virgin, Lantis. I can never make a baby as I will never experience sex.'

'What is sex?'

'Oh no. That one you can ask Zeus. He has the answers to your questions regarding sex and then some.'

'Is our father good at it?'

'I would not know. As I told you. I am a virgin.'

'I want to be a virgin also,' he told her with a smile. 'Just like you.'

Astraea smiled. She loved her little brother. His innocence reminded her off her own. Then she was sad to think of his fate. It was so tragic that his life would be so short. It was her father's plan and father knew what was best. He was king of the gods after all.

Astraea's thoughts were interrupted by a person approaching them in great haste. She recognised Ploutos. She hadn't seen him since the time she and her father saw him drunk in the street and Zeus had assisted him to sleep it off.

'I found you,' Ploutos declared.

'I see that you are not intoxicated?' Astraea observed sarcastically.

'I may never drink wine again. The end result is too damaging to my brain.'

'Who is this man? Lantis asked.

'This is Ploutos, Lantis. He is sort of our cousin,' she informed him.

'What is a cousin?'

'Our father has a sister and Ploutos is her son,' she tried to explain but Lantis just seemed confused.

'He does not know much, he is young,' she added by way of an explanation to Ploutos.

Suddenly, Ploutos grabbed Astraea shoulders and drew her toward him. He kissed her forcibly on the lips. In shock and indignation, Astraea pulled back and slapped him hard across the face.

His face reddened from the slap and he roared at her. 'Why did you hit me!'

'You assaulted me!' she retorted aggressively.

Ploutos raised his fist as if he were about to punch her, when the ground began to shake.

Astraea turned to Lantis who was standing still, but each muscle was tense. His face was reddening with rage.

'Run!' Astraea advised Ploutos whoes fear showed on his face.

He turned and ran for safety.

Lantis relaxed and the ground stopped shaking.

'I am sorry, Astraea. I was scared and then the ground started to move and I think it was me that did it.'

She held him tightly and protectively in her arms.

'You are my protector,' she told him reassuringly. 'And I love you all the more for it.'

She kissed his cheek.

Lantis was smiling happily as he took her hand and he held it for the remainder of their journey home.

***

Numerous worried petitioners now consulted with the goddesses about leaving their island.

Generally, when the people were confused as to what to do, or how to solve a problem, they would consult an oracle or a god. They would bring an offering or a gift of coin and food in exchange for insights in the solution to what troubled them. The Oracles were cautious about making an errors in their judgements as so the solutions they offered were often ambiguous. It was left up to the petitioner to work out the meaning of their response. The oracle was smart enough to protect themselves with answers that could not come back on them if they were wrong. Some oracles would make a great show of imbibing potions, often utilising harmless herbs, and they would burn incense to mystify the process.

When they consulted Themis, Astraea, Dike, or Nemesis, they did not do any of these things. They were told that they will be given a beverage to drink as they boarded the ships as they left the islands forever. The drink will calm any anxieties they have about leaving their homes and it will make the journey more pleasant.

What they were not been told was, that when they drink the water, they will lose all memory of ever having lived on the island. They will forget all of their distinctive customs, values, and traditions. They will forget that all men and women are equal and that each has right to freedoms of assembly, association, and inclusion, in the decision-making process. Their memories of what made Thera a unique and advanced society would be forgotten forever.

The four women were in demand for many days as many of the islanders sought counselling before boarding sailing ships that were bound for the mainland in the regions of Sparta and Athens.

***

'Lantis,' called Themis.

'Yes mother,' he replied as he entered the room.

Lantis was now fully grown. He looked, thought, talked, and behaved like a young man of twenty years old.

What are you doing?'

'I am going on a walk with Astraea,' he informed her.

'You and Astraea are remarkably close.'

'She has taught me many things, mother. We are best friends.'

'That is nice. I am glad she is a caring sister to you.'

'Dike and Nemesis are good to me also,' he defended.

'Yes, I know they are, but you do spend more time with Astraea, don't you?'

Lantis could see that she was smiling. He knew that meant that he was not in any trouble.

'I love her very much,' he informed her.

'Love! What do you know of love?' she demanded.

'Love is when you put the feelings and well-being of another person before your own.'

'That is one part of love,' she agreed.

'I must go now mother,' he told her.

She studied him without saying anything.

'Astraea is waiting!'

'Be safe my darling,' she advised him.

He turned and rushed out of the room.

'I love you!' she called.

'Me too!' he called back.

Lantis rushed into the entry parlour where Astraea was waiting for him. She had a hamper filled with food and a canteen of water.

'You ready?'

'Yes, I am,' he declared smiling and he seemed contented.

They left the building and headed for the coast. Today Astraea was going to teach Lantis to swim. He had seen other children swimming and wanted to experience it for himself.

They walked in silence for some time. 'I told mother that I love you,' he explained to Astraea.

'You are so sweet,' responded Astraea smiling. 'And I love you also.'

'So, it is true?' queried Lantis. He appeared puzzled.

'What is true? That you can love someone without wanting to have sex with them?'

'Yes, that is certainly true,' she explained. 'Sex is a part of a relationship between a man and his wife who yearn to make babies, and then they spend the rest of their lives together raising them as a family.'

'But the love a son has for his mother, or the love a brother has for his sister is different?'

'Yes,' she confirmed. 'It is still genuine love, but it is without the need for sex or any desire to make babies.'

'Our father has made many babies with his sister, Hera,' Lantis informed her.

Astraea said nothing. She turned pale.

Lantis knew that he had trapped her and he laughed. 'Astraea, I think our father is an exception to normal behaviour,' Lantis concluded

'He is indeed,' she hesitated and then laughed also.

Soon they had arrived at the beach.

'Do we swim naked?' he asked.

'It is more convenient if we do,' she agreed and they stripped off their clothing.

They had seen each other naked several times before, but it had recently occurred to Astraea that as Lantis developed into a man's body, his fascination with her body grew with it. She decided that the cold water would dampen any arousal he may inadvertently exhibit for her, and so she rushed into the water. Lantis ran in close behind her.

Standing neck deep in the water, they splashed happily and she dived under the water and swam away from him. He seemed worried when she could not be seen, and he was relieved when she surfaced.

He tried to duck his head under also, but he quickly reemerged spluttering.

She laughed. Hold your breath before you put your head under the water.

Lantis did so, and soon he was swimming both above the water and under the surface. They frolicked together in this way for some time.

'Astraea.'

'Yes, Lantis.'

'Do animals live in the ocean?'

'Yes many, why?'

'I know that fish do, as we have watched the fishermen bring them in, and you have explained fish to me. I have enjoyed eating the fish.'

'So why do you ask?'

'I have just seen a fish that appears to be bigger than a cow,' he told her. 'But it has no legs. Do cows live in the water?'

'As big as a cow!' she was alarmed. 'But it looked like a fish?'

'Yes, that is correct.'

'I think we had better leave the water,' she told him.

As they headed for the beach, a pod of dolphins breached the surface and performed for them squealing and squawking in playful delight.

Astraea laughed relieved. She towelled herself and dressed as did Lantis. She discreetly observed that the cold water had had the desired effect on his male member.

They talked some more as they ate their meal. Astraea loved spending time with her brother. Their talk was uninhibited and free flowing. He asked many questions about the gods, the humans, and bout human behaviour.

They then saw a man watching them from a distance. 'Is that Ploutos?' Lantis asked.

'I think so.'

Shall I shake the ground from under his feet?' he asked as if it were a casual trick to perform.

'Let us wait and see what he does first.'

Ploutos seemed to shrug his shoulders and he shuffled off.

'I fear that he is in Pothos's grasp,' she concluded.

Lantis looked at her and he appeared to not understand.

'Pothos is the God of sexual longing, yearning, and desire,' she explained.

Both Astraea and Lantis were quiet for a while in private contemplation. They had never really discussed his purpose, but she had learned that he now knew all about it. It was going to be dramatic and it would happen soon.

Lantis drew in a deep breath. 'Why do I have to do this?' he lamented.

'You are the son of Zeus, and he has decreed it.' she replied by way of an explanation.

In many ways she disliked her father for this. She now had a brother that she loved dearly. Soon she would lose him permanently, and she knew that she would forever have a saddened heart.

***

A group of humans were stood aside from the other evacuees. They had a defiant appearance about them.

'These people refuse to drink from the waters,' explained Acrisius to Zeus as he approached the commander and his soldiers.

'Then send them home,' Zeus ordered.

'But they do want to leave the island before it explodes.'

'Then they should drink the water,' Zeus replied calmly.

'They are becoming agitated,' Acrisius added.

'Then kill them,' Zeus said patiently. He was watching for the reaction on Acrisius face.

'My lord?'

Zeus decided to be patient. He explained calmly. 'If they do not drink, they cannot be evacuated. And if they do not leave, they will die on this island. Kill them now and be done with it. Make a public example of them,' explained Zeus. 'I am doing my best to spare their lives,' he added and was now becoming annoyed by these stubborn people who refused to follow his orders.

'But sire. I fear that may create a panic among those who are queuing responsibly to drink the water before they board the ships with their families...'

'Okay then, Commander, you carry on with your mission and I will personally deal with the trouble makers,' Zeus assured him.

Acrisius appeared to be relieved.

Zeus walked over to where the protesters were grouped. Several guards were nearby holding spears pointed at them, but they were clearly unsure of what they should do.

Zeus recognised Gorontalo, but although he recognised some of the others as the politicians that he had addressed only days earlier, he could not remember their names.

'Gorontalo, I see you there,' Zeus said to the assembled group.

'My lord, we do not want to drink that water!' he stated defiantly.

'Why not?' asked Zeus in concern.

'It is a trick,' offered someone.

'It is poison,' suggested another.

'Why would I poison you?' asked Zeus. If I wanted you to die, I would leave you here on the island to your fate.'

'We do not believe our island will explode,' someone argued.

'Did you not feel the earth shake?' Zeus demanded.

'It has shaken before,' came the reply.

'Fine, then stay here,' Zeus concluded and walked away. Zeus spoke to the guards as he passed them. 'Forcibly move these people to return to their homes. Use the pointy ends of your spears to hurry them along.'

The guards obeyed and headed for the trouble makers and the worrisome group hastily scattered.

'Zeus,' said a voice and he turned to see the four goddesses approach him. Lantis trailed slowly behind them. He was now fully grown, tall, muscular, and strikingly handsome with long blond hair.

'Ah, I am glad you are here. I wanted to check with you if you knew if my sister has left the island.'

'Apart from us here, all the other gods and goddesses have departed,' Themis assured him.

***

The day progressed and Zeus observed the remaining ships sail away with the breeze. He hoped that the people on them would be safe. He did not understand why they had not left sooner, as his instructions and warnings were very clear and specific.

Acrisius and his men were on the last ship. As arranged by Zeus, Lips, the God of the South West wind, was filling their sails and pushing them quickly away from the island and out of danger.

Zeus nodded his satisfaction. He turned to the women. 'It is time for you four to leave.'

'What about you?' Themis was concerned.

'I will fly back to Mount Olympus. I want to witness the event from up high.'

'May I join you?' Themis was weeping and Zeus readily capitulated recognising a mother's grief for her son.'

After a brief round of hugs, Dike and Nemesis transferred themselves directly to Mount Olympus. Only Astraea remained standing close to Lantis. They were holding hands.

***

Lantis was solemn as he embraced his mother for the last time. He hugged Astraea tightly and whispered in her ear, 'I love you so much.' He broke from their embrace, turned to Zeus and nodded. He smiled, did a meek wave, and turned to walk up the trail to the top of the mountain.

'Lantis!' Astraea called. 'Wait for me!'

Lantis stopped and turned. He could see Astraea hug the others, and she then ran up to him. 'I am coming with you,' she informed him with a smile.

'To make sure that I do not abandon my mission?' he asked as he shrugged, smiled, and nodded knowingly that he was accepting his fate.

'No, it is not that. I believe that you will complete your task,' she nodded at him. 'But I have decided that my time of living with humans is also coming to an end. I cannot start fresh with the memory of what is happening here,' she paused. 'The people of Thera have demonstrated that an inclusive, responsible society, can work and prosper, but our plans have been thwarted by the selfish need for gods to be unconditionally worshipped and for that they need to remain humble.' She drew in a deep breath and continued. 'I will use your fate to release me from immortality, and I will take my place in the heavens to be closer to my natural father.'

Together they climbed toward the summit. They trekked in silence and presently Lantis held Astraea's hand once more. She smiled, comforted by their bond. They turned and saw a giant eagle ascend from the island. Positioned on its back was her mother flying on Zeus to safety. Astraea wanted to wave, but she held herself back from doing so. She drew in a deep breath and examined Lantis. Lantis features had remained stoic and focused.

Astraea spotted the bridgeworks that they had only just started before Zeus's arrival. It had progressed without them, but it was still incomplete. She thought it ironic that it had seemed so important at the time, but now it would never be used. She pointed to the top of the mountain. 'Let's climb,' she suggested and they continued their ascent.

It took them nearly sixty minutes to reach the summit. They could see in the distance that some humans were still remaining in their villages, and some were at the port closing in on the boats that had not yet left. Astraea was somewhat surprised to realise that she did not care about their fate.

Lantis and Astraea then turned to each other. She drew back and held her arms high. In a clear bold voice, she declared. 'Behold what manner of race the fathers of the Golden Age left behind them! Far meaner than themselves! But you will breed viler progeny! Verily wars and cruel bloodshed shall be unto men, and grievous woe shall be laid upon them.'

'Goodbye cruel world,' Lantis added with a laugh.

'We cannot help them,' Astraea uttered as the tears streamed down her cheeks.

Astraea had to step further back from Lantis as he began to glow. The heat coming from him was suddenly intense. The ground began to shake violently. The explosion was sudden and enormous. As Lantis and Astraea vaporised, so did most of the mountain on which they stood. More than three quarters of the island blew apart, sending an enormous reddish-brown cloud of molten soil, rocks, and super-heated smoke into the air. The explosive cloud was so massive that it produced its own fierce storm of lightning bolts and thunder claps. If there were any witnesses, they would have explained it was "in honour of Zeus", but there were none. The people who had remained on the island all died at the same instant.

The explosion sent debris many thousands of metres into the sky. The deafening explosion shook homes on the island of Crete and Rhodes and the explosion could be heard by people as far away as Alexandra in Egypt, and Sparta on mainland Greece.

The ships that were sailing away from Thera felt the slight lift in the water beneath them as a giant wave passed beneath them. The enormous wave travelled fast and soon it swept over the lower islands hundreds of kilometres away at a furious speed. The tsunami claimed many lives and destroyed several coastal villages and drowned any inhabitants who were unlucky to be caught its destructive path.

Many days later the bulk of the dust began to settle. What remained of Thera was a smaller horseshoe shaped island and a scattering of smaller islets in the shape of a ring.

The crater that was formed by the blast still glowed hot in many places. All vegetation was gone. All the people, animals, birds, and even the insects were gone. Thera began a new period of time as a lifeless island. All that remained were the buried ruins of Themis's palace and parts of the stronger homes and public buildings. There were some remains of cooking ware, and implements that were used by the artisans, and some amphora's that had been stored in special underground vaults to maintain a steady temperature.

A message that was recently inscribed on a palace wall was now deeply buried by lava and ash, but it did partially survive the explosion. It was written by a loving, but grieving mother. I PRAY THAT LANTIS IS WELL REMEMBERED.

***

Sometime into their journey away from the island, Zeus and Themis heard the deafening noise of the explosion. Within a few moments they were briefly pushed forward by a massive gust of wind.

Zeus turned toward the boom, and he and Themis stared at the massive column of rocks and ash that rose high in the sky. It billowed at its peak the reddish-brown cloud was shaped like a giant mushroom. Lightening reached out in all directions.

Themis wept.

After several hours the eagle landed at Mount Olympus. Themis alighted and the eagle transformed back into Zeus.

He spoke calmly to the now assembling gods and goddesses. 'It is done.'

***

That night, a new constellation was formed in the starry heavens. Zeus named it "The Maiden" in honour of his newly adopted, but recently departed daughter, Astraea.

'She explained to me, that when humans return to a Golden Age, that she will give up her place in the heavens, and come back to us to walk and work once more with human's,' he paused. 'I look forward to her return.'

Those assembled did not speak. They stared into the night sky and in their own silent way, they paid homage to Astraea and the constellation that would eventually become known as "Virgo".

Demeter sat with Ploutos comforting her weeping son.

***

Several days later, the gods and goddesses of Mount Olympus were assembling in the great hall. It was nighttime and even Selene, Goddess of the moon, was present with orders not to shine tonight. No one wanted to miss the announcements that Zeus had for them. News, either good or bad, was always welcomed.

'I have had a meeting with Themis, Dike, and Nemesis,' he informed all those that were present. 'As a result, the following changes will take place immediately,' he explained and then added, 'Themis will step down from her involvement with humans. She believes she has weighed the evidence for and against conflicting parties for long enough.' He smiled at Themis who bowed her polite response.

'She has considerable skills and her judgments have always been fair and balanced. For this reason, we will now honour her for all eternity.'

When the applause died down, Zeus continued. 'As a symbol of her balanced and fair approach to life and justice, we have a new constellation in the heavens tonight. Observe "The scales", which is in honour of Themis and her balanced approach to justice,' Zeus pointed to the heavens and they cheered and clapped their approval.

In time, that constellation would become to be known to us as "Libra".

The immortals of Mount Olympus stared in wonder at the new constellation and they applauded Zeus's decision to elevate her in this way.

Themis then held up her hands and everyone settled and paid close attention. 'I have made peace with my daughters, Eunomia and Eirene. They will assist me,' she announced.

When calm returned, Zeus continued. 'Dike, is to be elevated to preside over the justice of mortals, and she will return to Athens with Athena to take up her role there. We wish her all the best,' he said as he looked at Dike.

'Yes father,' she replied happily.

Those gathering applauded once more.

'Nemesis will be traveling the mainland and will continue to seek out injustice and deliver retribution to those that deserve it.' Zeus informed everyone present. 'Oh, she informs me she is having a baby girl.'

'I have decided to name her Helen!' Nemesis called out. 'She will be so beautiful that men will fight over her!'

Everyone laughed, remembering what had happened with the Helen in the Trojan conflict.

And so, for a while, tranquillity was once again celebrated by the gods and goddesses of Mount Olympus. They fornicated, feasted, drank, and continued to play pranks on each other and the humans they presided over.

As always for the immortals of Mount Olympus, their peace would soon be disturbed. That however, is another story.

***

The Egyptian merchants sailed from Thera to their home in Alexandria with a fabulous new concept. They brought with them stamped coinage that increased the value of the coin by the multiple of the number minted on it. The ridicule that followed their presentation quickly killed their idea.

***

Two thousand four hundred years ago, a group of explorers beached their boat on the clean sands of the atoll. Their commander was named Aristocles, and he had wanted to explore the island since he was a teenager, from when he had heard tales from sailors that had seen abandoned homes and monuments on the island. He was intrigued enough to mount an expedition to explore these islands, and he was equipped to document what he saw. Armed with writing tablets and quills, he and his team commenced their search for any evidence of an ancient civilization.

Aristocles was already a highly regarded scholar, philosopher, and educator. His nick name was Plato, a name that was given to him by his wrestling coach. It was a name that stuck, and he was comfortable with it.

They nervously explored the island as during their brief time there, they felt numerous tremors. As much as Plato reassured his men, they remained pensive about exploring the island.

Plato himself came across the remains of what was once a stately home. It was mostly buried under rubble, but a recent landslide had cleared an opening. It looked too inviting to resist, and so he entered carrying a burning torch to light his way.

He marvelled at the frescos depicting a modern civilised culture. They were unquestionably old, and he didn't recognise their origins. He entered another room and saw writing on a wall. The left and right sides had crumbled away and only the mid-section remained. The words he read on the wall confused him. It read AT LANTIS. He immediately copied the lettering onto the tablet. The ground shook violently, and debris began to fall threatening him and his men with injury.

'Plato, it is an earthquake! We must leave here, now!' was the call from his leading hand. Reluctantly, Plato accepted the instruction to depart. He hurried out of the room just as rocks swept down a hill toward them. Plato managed to avoid the avalanche and his men escaped from the island without injury.

On the ship, Plato gathered his men closer to him and spoke is conspiratorial tones. 'This islands' location should forever remain a secret. If we ever speak of the wondrous world of Atlantis, we will say that it once existed beyond the pillars of Herakles, and that sadly, it sank beneath the waves before our very eyes.'

His men readily agreed, as they considered that place too dangerous to revisit.

The frescos and other objects that he had witnessed, as well as the lettering that he had copied from the wall, had captured Plato's imagination and it remained his preoccupation for the rest of his life. He loved embellishing the stories when describing what they had seen, but he continued to spread the disinformation about its location.

Plato had planned to return one day to complete his survey, but he never got to do so.

***

About two thousand years ago, an Egyptian Queen named Cleopatra had so much wealth, that her treasurer could not count it all. She met with her treasury staff to consult with them, and hopefully together they would decide on a solution.

'Perhaps we could build another vault,' was the recommendation.

'That will be expensive and it will fill too quickly.'

'You could spend some of it,' was another suggestion.

'I have everything I could ever want. The capital works programs that I am funding progress slowly for a lack of trades people. I cannot spend this money any faster.'

Cleopatra paced the room angrily. She came upon a door that she had not previously seen. 'What is behind that door?' she demanded.

'It is a vault where we store ancient coins. We were planning to re-mint them, but it has not been our priority,' the Chief Treasurer explained.

'Is the room large enough to store more of my wealth?' she asked, but without waiting for their reply, she opened the door and stepped inside.

Her torch bearers quickly followed her and lit up the room. She saw an old chest on a shelf on the wall, and she opened it up and peered inside. She saw ancient coins with numbers stamped on them and it gave her an idea.

Soon Cleopatra had devised a plan to insert a number ten digit onto all of her minted coin's thereby multiplying their value tenfold. Everyone agreed that it was a fabulous plan, and all the merchants and traders readily accepted the embossed coins and they immediately confirmed their stated value.

This great leap forward in owning portable wealth became so popular that it rapidly spread across the known world. Coincidentally, it is still in use today.

***

Present day - On the island of Santorini in the Aegean Sea.

Seismologists have warned that the earthquakes that have shaken the island might continue for many more months.

The majority of the island's inhabitants, and all of the tourists, have been evacuated off the island, for fear of either a major earthquake or a volcanic event that could be devastating to all life on the island. According to the head of the National Volcanic and Seismology

Warning Centre, the destruction could match the force of an event that had happened approximately 3,600 years ago. The only authorities to remain on the island are performing a door-to-door search of all homes and structures for any resistant home owners. Many of these homes have already been buffeted by hundreds of quakes that may end up rendering the island uninhabitable.

A group of searchers entered the remnants of the ancient palace with a sense of awe. The location of the palace had been unknown for thousands of years as it had been completely buried by an ancient seismic or volcanic event. Many of the ancient frescoes that survived on the walls were depicting scenes of fishermen, and farmers, and people playing games. A dust laden weaving loom featured in the centre of the room. The rest of the room was filled with pottery and jewellery and other ancient artifacts. On one wall both sides had partially caved in leaving only the middle of the wall intact.

One of the men who could read the ancient letters spelled it out in English. 'A T L A N T I S.'

His colleague stood beside him and asked. 'Do you think it is... a prank?' he speculated.

***

Novella one - the constellation Pisces

The Greek Constellation series of novellas by Stephan De Jonghe.

The ancient Greeks identified and named Forty-Eight out of the Eighty-Eight recognised constellations. They were catalogued by a Greek astronomer Claudius Ptolemy in his publication the Almagest around 150 CE. The origins of the mythological stories that identified the constellations predate this documentation by as much as a thousand years.

Novella one - the constellation Pisces and the story of Aphrodite and Eros, the Two Fishes.

Aphrodite is well known as the Greek goddess of love, romance, and sexuality. Aphrodite is also known to us as   Venus, and the planet is named after her in her   honour. This is the story of how Aphrodite came to be. Born in the ocean during a struggle between father and son, she was raised on an island. As an adult she was carried by Zeus to Mount Olympus to work and play with the gods and goddesses who resided there.

After a brief marriage to Hephaestus, she formed a steamy relationship with Hephaestus's brother, Ares and they had a son they named Eros. All her life, she struggled with the unwanted, yet amorous advances of the Titan monster named, Typhon. Eventually, she and Eros had to flee Mount Olympus to escape his wrath, and they eventually became the constellation of the Two Fishes, known to us as Pisces.

This book is now also available as a Paperback and Ebook

Novella two – the constellation of Capricorn

Novella two – the constellation of Capricorn and the story of Pricus the Sea-Goat.

Pricus is an old sea-goat with a problem. He is regarded as the old man of the sea. The younger generation wants desperately to abandon the old ways and leave their ocean home to live a more adventurous life on the land. The sea-goats are able to morph from sea-goats into land goats when they emerge from the surf to walk on land. They quickly learn to morph into human form, and to their delight discover that they can have much more fun exploring the plethora of opportunities that await them. In their naivety they make many mistakes, some ending in tragedy. Pricus is desperate to save the younger generation from themselves, and so must become increasingly resourceful do so, and do so in a way that his solution stays permanent. His dedication to his own kind earns him his place as the constellation of the sea-goat, known to us as Capricornus or Capricorn.

Planned launch 2026

Novella three - Saturn's moon Pandora

Novella three - Saturn's moon Pandora and the story of the first human woman.

Zeus, king of the Greek God's, commissioned his son Hephaestus to craft the first human woman. Aided by Athena, he carefully researched the perfect form and then moulded her from clay He then painted and glazed her into the perfect woman. After being fired in his kiln, she was given the breath of life by the wind god Zephyr. She was named Pandora, being the bearer of the gifts bequeathed to her by the gods and goddesses of Mount Olympus. Her main purpose for humanity was to become the role model for all future human women. Zeus then commanded that she be properly trained so that she can navigate life's complexities, but her tutors do too good a job with her, and she becomes too powerful for a normal human life. Zeus became disillusioned with her and he decided that she should be married off to a minor god, so that she'll do no harm to herself, or to others.

Pandora's story is so significant that she is honoured as Pandora, one of Saturn's moons.

This book is now available in both paperback and Ebook

Novella four - the constellation Taurus

Novella four - the constellation Taurus and the story of the Jupiter's moon Europa and her meeting with the white bull.

When Zeus, king and master of the gods and goddesses of Mount Olympus finds himself between wives he sets out on a desperate search for the perfect woman to marry. On a sunny field, set among spring flowers, on a stretch of land adjacent to the sea, he finds her. She is Europa, a gorgeous African princess. For Zeus, it becomes love at first sight. In his infatuation for this woman, he tries numerous times to impress her, and almost succeeds. Sadly, for Zeus, his one true love is betrothed to another, and sadly for Zeus, a daughter must do her duty. Disguised as a magnificent white bull, he tries one last desperate attempt to have her. The consequences of his quest for true love are celebrated as the constellation of the white bull, know to us as the Taurus.

Also commemorated in this story is the constellation Draco, known as Ladon the Dragon. Also featured is Laelaps as the constellation Canis Major or Greater Dog, and the Teumessian Fox as the constellation Canis Minor or Lesser Dog.

This book is now available in paperback and Ebook

Novella five- the constellations Scorpio and Orion

Novella five- the constellations Scorpio and Orion and the story of the scorpion verses the hunter.

Artemis is the goddess of the forests and of the hunt. She befriends a hunter named Orion. Their friendship is slowly progressing toward a blossoming romance when Orion boasts of his ability to wantonly kill all the animals that cross his path. Artemis is dismayed. Her policy is to only kill for food, to kill for pleasure is an outrage. She feels she must sacrifice her future relationship by stopping Orion from completing his boast. She manifests a giant scorpion and sends it to attack and destroy Orion. A massive battle ensues and both are defeated, thus preserving animal life from indiscriminate killings. To celebrate the outcome and to remind us that all life is precious, their images are cast into the heavens as the constellation *Orion* and the constellation of the Scorpion known to us as *Scorpio*.

Planned launch 2025

Novella six - the constellation Aries

Novella six - the constellation Aries and the story of Chrysoma-llos the Ram.

Born from a union between Poseidon and Theophane on a remote island that was the home of a flock of sheep. They are interrupted by shepherds during copulation, so they disguised themselves as sheep to avoid the embarrassment that Theophane might suffer if their tryst became public knowledge. Their male child is born with the ability to morph from human form into a ram. From his father, he has long golden hair, and when he becomes a ram, he has golden fleece. He has wings and the ability to fly.

He is named Chrysomallos and he is raised by his loving mother Theophane. He eventually befriends princess Helle who live in a nearby kingdom. When their lives become perilous, Chrysomallos the flying, golden fleeced Ram, comes to their rescue. His bravery is celebrated as the constellation of the Ram, know to us as *Aries*.

This book is now available in both Paperback and Ebook

Novella seven - the constellation of Ophiuchus

Novella seven - the constellation of Ophiuchus and the story of Asclepius the serpentius or serpent bearer.

Asclepius was the son of Apollo. When Apollo had to rescue Asclepius from his dying mother's womb, he realised that he did not know enough about medicine and surgery, and so he set about discovering as much as he could. He later taught all that he learned to his son. Next, to further his education, Apollo decided that Asclepius would learn even more from the tutor Chiron. Through him he completed his training and went on to be the foremost authority on how to manage illness and repair injuries. His wife Epione and he had five daughters and three sons, and all became involved in the practice of medical treatments. The most prominent daughter was Hygieia and the practice of hygiene is named after her.

Both Apollo and Asclepius have been forever revered as the fathers of medical treatments and their names were included in the original Hippocratic Oath, that all medical practitioners swore upon when becoming formally registered to become doctors.

His dedication to healing the sick and injured was commemorated in the night sky as the constellation *Ophiuchus*. Many people who practice in astrology believe that Ophiuchus is the unrecognised thirteenth star sign.

Also featured is the constellation of *Serpens* or "The Snake," who Asclepius witnessed bringing healing herbs to another snake who was sick, and this event started him on his discovery of benefits of medicinal herbs.

Planned launch 2026

Novella eight - the constellations of Cancer & Leo

Novella eight - the constellations of Cancer & Leo and the stories of Karkinos the giant crab, Zosma the Nemean lioness, Astron the hydra, Aquila the eagle, Sagitta the arrow, and the constellation named after Herakles the Demi-God.

The birth of Herakles was surrounded by controversy. Being the demi-god son of the King of all the gods, he found it difficult to live a routine life with his wife and children.

Herakles was persecuted by Hera for being her husband Zeus's illegitimate son, and so he was inflicted by incessant painful headaches. He was told of a remedy by the oracle in Delphi, but before he could be cured, it required him to agree to take on many incredible tasks which were assigned to him by the local king. By completing these labours, he should be able to go on to live a long and fulfilling life.

He later became immortal, and Herakles is forever remembered as a Greek Mythological hero for defeating the giant crab that became known as constellation Cancer. He also killed the man-eating lioness that became known as the constellation Leo. He slew the serpent of Lake Lerna, which is now known as the constellation Hydra. Herakles used an arrow now known as the constellation Sagitta to kill a giant eagle that became to be known as the constellation Aquila or "The Eagle".

Herakles was finally accepted at Mount Olympus and wa s honoured with the constellation Herakles also known as Hercules.

This book is now available in Paperback and Ebook

Novella nine - the constellation Gemini

Novella nine - the constellation Gemini and the story of the twins, Castor and Polydeuces.

Leucippe was desperate to become a grandmother. Fed up with her son-in-law's lack of progress, she asked Zeus for help. When Zeus arrived, he took the opportunity, disguised himself as a swan, and then he did much more than just arrange for Leda to become pregnant.

The Spartan twins grew up to become skilled horsemen, hunters, warriors, and adventurers. They embarked on many journeys together and their adventures included sailing on the Argo with Jason on his quest for the golden fleece, being hunters at the Calydonian wild boar hunt, and fighting Trojans at Troy. It was their sister Helen, who was the central reason for that protracted war.

The twins were honoured by Zeus for their bravery and commitment to each other, and he cast their image into the night sky to be forever remembered as the constellation of the Twins, which is now known as *Gemini*. Also featured in this story is the constellation The Swan or *Cygnus*.

This book is now available in Paperback and E book

Novella ten - the constellations of Virgo & Libra

Novella ten - the constellations of Virgo & Libra and the story of the Astraea the maiden, and Themis the scales.

Astraea and Themis were both goddesses who were committed to advancing the living conditions of the humans who lived on the island of Thera. Along with other gods and goddess they believed that they'd become the role models for all future human progress advancements.

Astraea strongly believed in justice and sort punishment for those that transgressed against the common good. Her belief was that punishment was a deterrent and that the formal process of trial and conviction for those found guilty of a crime had a place in society.

Themis was more about bringing about restitution to an aggrieved person who was treated unfairly by another. He mediation skills gave rise to the belief that there was always a remedy when agreements fell apart.

However, the speed of their progress and their intentions to achieve self-determination worried Zeus. After inspecting the work and assessing all that had been achieved, he concluded that it must come to an abrupt end. And as every Greek immortal knows, when

Zeus is determined and has made up his mind, nothing stops it his decision from happening. For Astraea the decision was devastating, so she cast herself into the night sky as "the maiden", forever watching over humanity as the constellation *Virgo*.

Themis was later honoured for her balanced outlook on life and is remembered as the scales as she evenly balanced out her reasoning and decisions. She is now known to us as the constellation *Libra*.

This book is now available in Paperback and E Book

Novella eleven – the constellation Aquarius

Novella eleven – the constellation Aquarius and the story of Ganymede the water bearer.

Ganymede was adopted by a family of shepherds when he was found abandoned as a young child. He preferred his own company, and whilst good at caring for the sheep he was regarded as a misfit by his adopted family.

One day, as he was tending the sheep, he was spotted by Zeus, who flying past in his eagle form. Out of curiosity Zeus landed to meet the young man and became quickly enamoured with him. Ganymede found himself attracted to the powerful God and very much wanted to be with him. Zeus easily convinced the young man to give up his shepherding life and come with him to Mount Olympus.

Ganymede became Zeus's friend and lover. He took over the role of cup bearer during important civil functions from Zeus's daughter Hebe, as she had found love and married a Greek Hero. Ganymede quickly became fascinated with aqueducts and fountains, and he was responsible for improving the water quality and availability of clean drinking water to Mount Olympus's inhabitants. His contribution is celebrated as the constellation of the "water bearer" now know to us as **Aquarius.**

Planned launch 2025

Novella twelve – the constellation of Sagittarius

Novella twelve – the constellation of Sagittarius and the story of the "Archer" Crotus.

A water Naiad nymph named Eupheme was a demi-goddess of the Hippocrene freshwater spring near Mount Helicon. She was youthful, very beautiful, and powerful. She met and had a relationship with the God Pan, a Satyr, famous for playing the pipes was the god of shepherds, flocks, rustic musicians, and improvisation. Their romance led to the birth of Crotus.

Crotus was a Satyr and grew up to be like his like his father, preferring the company of muses. Most Satyrs preferred the company of Dionysus, God of wine, revelry, and debauchery, so Crotus was unusual in this way.

The muses were providers of inspiration to artists, musicians, poets, story tellers, artisans, entertainers, and dancers. They brought out the natural talents of those they inspired, and positively encouraged them to excel by pursuing their passions and striving for perfection in their chosen art form.

Crotus was also a great hunter, and many say that he invented the hunting bow. He was more popular as a musician and his most noteworthy contribution to   performance music was the addition of rhythmic beats used to accompany the musician's musical score. He was also responsible for the introduction of a ritual applause to signify both pleasure from the performance and gratitude to the artist for their dedication to the composition and the quality of the performance. The applause was widely recognised as a significant motivator for artistic excellence.

Crotus was a mortal, and when he died, the Younger Muses petitioned Zeus to have his likeness immortalised as place in the night sky. Their petition was positively received, and, in his honour, he created the constellation of the Archer which is known to us as **Sagittarius**.

Planned launch 2026

Novella thirteen – the constellation Centaurus

Novella thirteen – the constellation Centaurus and the story of the tutor Cheiron.

Cheiron was a centaur who became the tutor to many of the legendary heroes of Greek mythology. Unlike other centaurs, Cheiron was intelligent, civilised and very kind. He was the teacher of students that included Jason, Castor, Polydeuces, Asclepius, Peleus, and Achilles and he taught them philosophy, archery, hunting, medicine, music, gymnastics, and the art of prophecy.

His life ended tragically when he was accidently struck with a poisoned arrow by his close friend, Herakles. Herakles had loosed the arrow in an attempt to ward off marauding cruel centaurs who came to cause mischief to Cheiron, but in the confusion, Cheiron stepped into the path of the arrow and was stuck. His immortality prevented his death, but the strong   poison caused him everlasting agony. He decided to surrender his immortality to Zeus so that he could pass into the underworld. He was then commemorated as the constellation of the Centaur and is known to us as **Centaurus.**

Planned launch 2025

The other Greek constellations that are yet to be featured include Andromeda, Ara, Auriga, Boötes, Cassiopeia, Cepheus, Corona Australis, Corona Borealis, Corvus, Crater, Delphinus, Equuleus, Eridanus, Lepus, Lupus, Lyra, Pegasus, Perseus, Piscis, Austrinus, Triangulum, Ursa Major, Ursa Minor, and Argo Navis (now divided into Carina, Puppis, and Vela)

Follicle Farm – A novel adventure

Follicle Farm – A novel adventure. (Fiction)

Follicle Farm is a comical and imaginative insight into organisational structure and behaviour of the trillions of cells that make up the microscopic world of every living person. It reveals how cells within the human body really think and how they, mostly, work well together. Bobby is a Mitochondria, and he works as a humble Follicle Farmer. He, with millions of colleagues, are part of the amazing organisation dedicated to growing hair for the human male that they live inside of. Recently, Bobby made an important discovery when he learned how to reverse the effects of alopecia and greying hair. Now it's up to management to debate if they should use his technique.

Join Bobby as he travels the body, ably assisted by Banjo and Skip, as he meets and deals with other human cells in various systems throughout the body. Bobby quickly learns there is more to management than just servicing the body's needs. Cliques, quirks, politics, unions, and hidden agendas, all thrive in Bobby's world.

You'll share in his adventure of personal growth as he encourages other Follicle Farmers to utilises best practices in growing quality hair.

This book is now available in Paperback and E Book

Your concise guide to the meaning of life

Your concise guide to the meaning of life. (Non-Fiction)

This is a serious book designed to help people. Its main purpose is to assist you on how to gain insights on how to live a happier and more fulfilled life. It will give you, the reader, instant benefits. It is peppered with many great quotes, many of them are my own. I've combined my interest in philosophy, sociology, psychology, and history to delve into the true meaning of life. The reader will not only understand why they are here, but how to make their experience more meaningful.

My main aim is to inspire readers into taking more control of how they make decisions that positively affect their achievements, successes, happiness, and therefore their well-being. The book is a summary of concise points that are easy to learn and apply to the readers life for an immediate benefit. It includes popular relevant quotes to re-enforce the messages and teaching. I have also included personal anecdotes that give real life and meaningful examples of how the material applies to all readers.

Topics include
- an explanation the main purpose for living.
- how to improve your relationships.
- how communication works and how to make it more effective.

- understanding your needs and desires and
  how to improve outcomes for yourself.
- understanding what motivates other people.
- how to exceed your own expectations.
- understanding your own personal legal,
  moral, ethical, and value system.
- improving your control over your emotions.
- understanding the concepts of faith,
  fate and fairness.
- and being better prepared for the
  final stages of your life.

This book is now available in Paperback or E-Book